The Lunchbox

The Lunchbox

A Collection of Short Stories

by

A.L. (Elle) Fredine

ISBN: 978-1-962077-17-0

Contents

Is this the way the world ends?

Scary and Other Fairy Tales

A Box of Chocolates

Featured

Always Put Your Best Foot Forward

When meeting new people, you should always put your best foot forward---though, sometimes you might need a little help from a friend

"Hey. My name is Caledonia Greengrass. Please-ta-meetcha." Callie squinted at her reflection in the fly-specked, wavering glass. What she saw staring back didn't fill her with confidence: baby-fine, mouse-brown hair skinned back in wispy French-braids; down-turned, apologetic, hazel eyes; and a small, pink, rosebud mouth, poised to beg pardon for whatever'd just passed its lips.

"Such a sweet li'l mouth --- a perfec' cupid's bow," her ma always said. Too bad cupid's bows were last in style twenty years ago.

The girl in the mirror peered back at Cassie. Her lathe-thin body was enveloped in a worn but freshly-pressed pink-and-red-striped cotton dress printed on the skirt pockets with smiling cat faces. White knee-socks drooped on her skinny legs and balled up under too-narrow feet. Deep cracks in her leather saddle-shoes showed through their thick coat of polish.

The uneven hem of her hand-knit sweater sagged on one side, and the baggy left sleeve was over-long. Whoever'd knitted it had chosen a shade of crusty, festering, mustard-yellow, guaranteed to suit no-one on this earth.

Callie sighed. She knew Ma had done her best to find something nice for Callie's first day at her new school. But fifty-cents, though a considerable sum to Callie and her ma, really don't go far, even in a church-basement jumble sale. And Ma's color-sense was iffy on a good day. This hadn't been one.

Maybe the teacher would excuse her from introducing herself to the class. Take pity on the new kid. Fat chance.

Callie would've been fine staying at St. Mary's. She was happy there. Though it served the poorest families in the parish, the school had a fine reputation. But Ma was convinced the only way her daughter would have a chance at a college education was through a scholarship from Miss Lydia Farmer's Academy for Young Women. And when her ma made up her mind, well, there was no getting around it.

So, with Callie's excellent academic record, and a glowing letter of recommendation straight from the hand of the Arch-Bishop of the Diocese, the girl was admitted to Miss Lydia's fall term as a Special Student. Only a few 'special' girls had ever been accepted in the long, proud history of the academy --- three since its founding in eighteen-and-forty-seven, almost a full hundred years. Callie would be the fourth.

She stuffed her hand-painted, wooden pencil case into her satchel, along with six new scribblers. Now, that had been a find! A cellophane-wrapped pack for only a dime. Mind you, they were thin, and the paper was poor quality, but they were new and to Callie's eyes, perfect.

She gazed around the room she shared with her mother at the top of the great house. Formerly the maids' quarters, it had been refurbished for Callie and her ma. When they'd first moved in, Miz Carter'd been at great pains to explain as how her cook usually had a room off the kitchen, but she'd made this arrangement special for them. Callie was pretty sure the real reason had been Miz Carter didn't want a little kid underfoot downstairs.

The tiny bedroom alcoves under the eaves on either side could be closed off from the sitting room by privacy curtains. An ancient horse-hair-stuffed sofa squatted on carved, wooden feet under the oval, tilt-frame window. The sofa was sided by two elderly wing chairs --- good, solid pieces but well past their prime, cast-offs from the downstairs parlor when Miz Carter had it 'redone' in a new style she favored, Danish Modern, or, as Miz Carter said, "Mow-dern."

Callie privately thought it cold and severe, but it made her Saturday mornings easier. Wiping down a few tall, skinny lamps and dusting the sleek, bare, teak tables was nothing compared to hand cleaning each bit of China bric-a-brac which had cluttered up the old, Victorian-style parlor.

"You are my sunshine, my only sunshine..."

Callie hummed the popular tune as she clattered down the steep, back stairs to the kitchen. The bright fall morning poured in through high, multi-paned windows and drizzled butterscotch on the day. Fresh, oblongs of dough warm from the proofing oven marched in a neat, soldierly row across crisp, linen tea-towels on the scrubbed-pine table, waiting for Callie's ma to punch them down one last time and pop them into the huge, shiny, black oven.

Her ma turned from the stack of bread pans soaking in the stone sink under the windows and raised a sudsy hand in warning. "Hush your racket, chil'. Miz Carter's still sleepin' an' Miss Claire ain' come down yet."

Callie grinned. In all the time she and her ma had 'done' for the Carters, she'd never know either one to surface before ten. Miz Carter always took her coffee in the morning room, with its view of her beloved rose garden. And Miss

Claire never graced the dinner table before luncheon.

Callie set her satchel by the door and hugged her ma. She'd tied up her long dark hair in one of her colorful turbans and she smelled of yeast and lemony dish-soap. A stray bubble tickled Callie's nose.

Her ma took the girl by the shoulders, her sparkling brown eyes locked on her daughter's timid gaze. "You ready, chil'?"

Ma's voice was warm and spicy, just like her Creole gumbo, thick with love and hot-peppers. "Jus' put your best foot forward, an' you'll be fine." She cupped a wet hand under Callie's chin. "No slouchin', now. Y'all stan' up tall. Greengrass is a proud, old N'O'leans family..."

Callie thrust her shoulders back. "Yes'm. I remember... descended from Édouard Gingras, the Acadian, expelled by the British to roam the south 'til he found a home with Jean Lafitte, deep in the everglades."

Ma nodded, pleased with her daughter's recitation. Callie gazed at her mother's petite frame, well-padded and womanly in all the right places. "I wish..."

"An' what would your Nana Selina say 'bout wishin' yourself away."

Callie giggled. Some of her favorite memories were of her tiny, wizened grandmother, rocking by a big open fireplace, dispensing hugs an' home-spun wisdom in equal proportions. The saying her ma referred to, "If wishes were horses, the beggars'd ride," in Nana Selina's mouth, was more pungent than polite, but all the more memorable. "Weesh in one 'and, sheet in one 'and, clap zem, so! An' what you 'ave?"

Her ma took two ham-salad biscuits, left-over from yesterday's lunch, and wrapped them in waxed paper. She popped them in a brown paper sac and added slice of sharp cheddar, a jam-tart and a small apple. 'That oughta keep you 'til supper. Scoot, now. An' don't go bangin' the door. I got a seed cake in th' oven."

Callie closed the door soft as a fox slidin' quiet past a sleepin' hound-dog's nose. She managed to keep her spirits up all the way to the old bridge at Fortnum Road. Once across, the dirt lane divided. One fork wound down through sunlit pastures towards town and dear, familiar St. Mary's. The other climbed the hill where massive, white oaks cast their cool, dappled shade across the road to Miss Lydia's.

Callie stared at the sunny lane, thinking how wonderful it would be to skip down it and join her friends at St Mary's, where she wouldn't have to face a room full of strangers---worse, a room full of strangers from fine homes where girls like Callie made their beds and picked up after them, washed their dirty laundry, cleaned their bathrooms.

Ma's voice rang in her ears. Put yer best foot forward. Callie squared her shoulders, and trudged up the drive towards the wrought-iron gates.

Footsteps crunched in the gravel behind her. Startled, Callie swung round and eyed the approaching trio.

A sharp-eyed, raven haired girl loomed over Callie. "You lost?" Her friends snickered.

Callie shook her head.

"Well, then, you better git."

"But --- but I'm a new student, here."

"Here?" The girl's lip curled. "You don't belong here." She wrenched Callie's satchel from her hands and threw it into the lane, then shoved Callie after it.

Callie tripped and landed hard. The dark-haired girl and her friends sauntered away. Their careless laughter floated back on the cool morning air. "Welcome to Miss Lydia's, New Girl."

Callie sat on the grassy verge and picked gravel out of her knee and wished with all her might she could just fly away to St Mary's.

The blare of a car-horn made her jump. Miss Claire, a pale, chiffon scarf protecting her perfect auburn curls, wheeled her sleek, two-seater roadster to a halt beside Callie. "Get in."

Callie fanned away the billowing dust and stared, bemused. "Who, me?"

"You see someone else sittin' by the road? Get in, you'll be late for class."

"I'm not goin' to that school. I can't." To her horror, Callie's voice trembled.

"Yes, you can. An' you will." Claire nodded towards Callie's skinned knee. "You hurt?"

"Not much."

"Then get in."

Callie retrieved her satchel and slid into the passenger seat, the smooth leather cool against her legs. Miss Clare put the convertible in gear and rocketed up the lane. The young woman watched Cassie from the corner of her eye, but the girl was too sunk in misery to notice her surroundings.

Lush manicured lawns surrounded the gracious, Georgian-style stone buildings. Beds bursting with vibrant mums, violas and purple asters lined curving walkways, and tall urns crammed with scarlet geraniums and English ivy framed the portico.

The sleek roadster swept up the broad, circular drive and rolled to a stop by the grassy common. Claire surveyed the clusters of girls on their way to class. "Who's queen-bee this year?" She drummed long, scarlet nails on the steering wheel.

Her gaze sharpened. She pulled her sunglasses down and stared over the rims at a slim, blonde girl in a pale blue cashmere twin-set over a cream pencil-skirt, the epicenter of a fawning circle of younger girls. "Perfect."

Claire poked Callie's arm. "You hush, now, and learn." She summoned a toothy smile and waved. "Yoo-hoo. Bootsie --- Bootsie Warren."

Callie stared but sat quiet.

Puzzled but curious, the blonde girl approached the roadster. Her little coterie followed at a respectful distance.

"Bootsie Warren, jus' look at you. Las' time I set eyes on you, you were all freckles an' gangly knees --- an' those braces --- my, my, my. You get them off yet?" Claire's smile broadened. "You don't remember me, do you, Bootsie. I'm Claire, Claire Carter. I went here with your older sister, Beckie. We were such friends. Why, we even dated the same boy, Roger Somebody... I forget now, Roger... what was his name?"

The girl stiffened. Her cheeks flushed bright pink. "I'm sure I don't recall."

"Well, no matter. This here's our cook's daughter, Callie Greengrass. Callie, say, 'Hi,' to Bootsie."

Callie ducked her head in a shy smile. "Um...Hi, Bootsie."

The blonde girl's eyes glinted. "My name is Beth-Ann. Only my friends call me 'Bootsie'."

Claire flapped a careless hand, waving away Beth-Ann's protest. "Oh, Bootsie, I jus' know Callie's gonna do real well here with you in her corner. Don't you agree? Oh, an' say 'Hi,' to Becky for me."

The blonde girl smiled as if her face hurt. "Callie. Nice to meet you, I'm sure." She stalked away, her back poker-straight.

Claire tapped a tailor-made against her enameled case and thumbed the wheel on her heavy, gold lighter. She sucked in a lung-full of smoke and let it trickle out her nose.

"Beth-Ann's sister, Beckie? Roger Cunningham got her pregnant our senior year. I heard they sent her back east to an auntie or some such." She flashed a stern glance at Callie. "Beth-Ann'll be nice or, at least, ignore you as long as you don't let on you know anythin'. So, forget what I jus' tol' you an' don't ever say a word about her sister. Understand?"

Callie shook her head. "No'm."

Claire sighed. "Listen. Now Beth-Ann knows I've taken an interest in you, she an' her bunch will leave you be. She doesn't dare mess with me, but that only goes so far. The second you act like you have somethin' over her, she'll make it her life's work to rid this town of you an' your mama. Got it?"

Callie nodded.

"Good. Now get to class."

"Yes'm." Callie slid out of the roadster clutching her satchel and paused, her hand on the door. "Um, thank you, Miss Claire."

Claire snorted. "Don't thank me. Jus' prove your mama right. Go to college. Use your brain for somethin' besides holdin' your ears apart."

She spun the roadster round, spraying dust and gravel. Her cheeky horn blared, drawing every eye. Then Claire waved and shouted over her shoulder before she sped off. "See you tonight, Callie."

Curious girls, including a tall, brown-eyed one with raven hair, stared after the sports car, wondering who this new student was to rate such attention from the stylish and much-envied Miss Claire Carter.

A tiny smile lifted the corners of Callie's lips as she hurried to meet her new class-mates. Maybe this wouldn't be such a bad First Day, after all.

• • •

Spelling Bee

Sometimes, the answer's right under your nose, but you need a friend to point it out.

"Ruthie? You comin', Ruthie?"

Silence.

"Ruth-Ann!"

Ruth-Ann stared out her bedroom window at the brilliant, cloudless, May morning while her mama banged about downstairs.

"Ruth-Ann! You git yourself down here. I'm about to melt, slavin' over this hot stove."

Ruth-Ann pictured her mama, red-faced, buzzin' 'round the kitchen while bacon sizzled in the cast-iron skillet and cream-o-wheat bubbled in the little, brown porridge pot. Though, why her mama believed a body would want porridge on a day this hot was beyond Ruth-Ann.

The air was already fierce, though 'twas barely spring. Summer'd be a scorcher, for sure.

She wondered if she let her mamma holler long enough, would she actually melt?

Ruth-Ann sighed. Having heard that particular threat on many occasions in her eight years, she decided it likely wouldn't happen this time, either.

She crossed her ankles and regarded her shiny, patent-leather shoes.

Mama had got 'em from the church jumble sale, but they were barely scuffed. Only one, teensy scratch across the toe-cap of the left shoe. You couldn't hardly see it 'less you got real close.

"Lookit these, Sissy. Shiny as a new penny," Mama had said, holdin' the shoes up, proud as if she'd won first prize at the fair.

"Sissy." That's what Mama called Ruth-Ann when she was extra-pleased. Most of the time though, it was just plain "Ruthie."

Ruth-Ann smoothed her freshly-pressed pinnie over thin, sun-browned knees and swung her feet.

A soft *pat-a-pat* at the window dragged her attention away from the shiny patent-leather. She hopped off her bed and skipped across the faded, red rag-rug for a better look at her visitor.

Ruth-Ann smiled at the fat bumblebee bumping against the glass. As she raised the sash, her curtains ruffled in the warm breeze.

The bumblebee waddled over the sill, then flew straight to the pile of books on Ruth-Ann's bed-side table.

Ruth-Ann crouched on the floor by her bed, watching the bee explore the cover of the topmost volume. "*Treasure Island*'s a good book," she said. "Though, I do believe the writer would'a done better to make Jim Hawkins a girl. It'd be nice for girls to have grand adventures, too."

Her guest bumbled aloft and made a bee-line for Ruth-Ann's bookshelf, where it buzzed up and down the spines, as if looking for one in particular.

It perched for a moment atop "National Velvet."

"Oh, yes, that's a fine girl-story," said Ruth-Ann. "But I'd rather be a pirate than a jockey."

The bee settled on a thin, red-bound school-book.

Ruth-Ann pulled it out, careful not to disturb its fuzzy passenger, and placed the book on her bed.

The slim, red volume fell open to a well-marked spot. The bee trundled across the pages, stopping here, then there, circling back, then moving on. Several times it flew up, only to light again in the same word.

Ruth-Ann laughed. "Aren't you smart. I was studyin' those all las' night. But, you better shoo, before Mama comes. She don't care much for 'insecks'."

The bumblebee circled the pages one last time, then zoomed out the window just as Ruth-Ann's mama burst into her room.

"Stop yer day-dreamin'. Breakfast's ready an' you can't be late --- not today of all days."

By ten-thirty, though, Mama's fine breakfast had turned into a lead ball in Ruth-Ann's stomach. Worse, every time Ruth-Ann mind drifted to the coming face-off with her fourth-grade nemesis, Mary McConnell, the heavy, lumpen ball started in with such a flip-floppin', it threatened to come back up.

And, no matter how hard she willed it to stop, the clock at the front of the classroom kept right on tickin' off the minutes.

Big, fat drops of sweat trickled between Ruth-Ann's shoulder-blades and oozed down her back. Her legs stuck to the hard, wooden seat.

She squirmed just as her seat-mate, Ardith Jones, was about to dip her pen in their shared ink-well.

Ardith hissed under her breath. "You make me blot my book, an' I'll smack you upside the head at recess."

Ruth-Ann froze. She an' Ardith were companionable enough, but Ruth-Ann had to admit, they weren't exac'ly best friends. Besides, Ardith was two inches taller and outweighed Ruth-Ann by a good ten pound, mebbe more. A smack upside the head from Ardith would hurt.

Ruth-Ann inched away as far as she could without falling off the seat.

Then, the very next minute, it seemed, she was standing at the front of the room beside Mary McConnell.

What...?

Ruth-Ann had no memory of recess, of lunch, in fact, of anything at all since that mornin'. She wished the buzzing in her ears would stop. It was makin' it hard for her to work out what'd happened.

The buzz became a voice. "Ruth-Ann, do you wish to hear your word again?"

Mrs. Turnbuckle tone was as mild as always. Not that she ever needed to raise her voice. She could flay the skin off a malefactor from twenty paces with her most genteel murmur.

But, standin' at the back of the closed, stuffy room as she was, Mrs. Turnbuckle did sound a teensy bit annoyed. And, what teacher wouldn't, tryin' to show off for the principal, an' one of her prize spellers chokes.

Oh, shoot. Ruth-Ann knew where she was now. She glanced to her right. Yup, there he was, sitting at Mrs. Turnbuckle's desk. Principal

Hardisty, pince-nez clamped on the bridge of his long, thin nose.

Ruth-Ann gulped. "Ma'am?"

"Do you wish to hear your word again? Or would you like to pass?"

Pass? Might as well lay down dead right now as give a word to Mary McConnell. "No'm. Can I --- I mean, may I hear my word again?"

The match ground on. Word followed word, some faster'n a blink, some slow as a dew-worm inchin' 'cross a dry creek-bed.

Both girl watched, lynx-eyed, each waiting for the other to slip. Quarter was neither asked nor given. Sudden-death elimination stalked the room.

Polite applause gave way to strained silence as the entire fourth-grade class held its breath. Who'd be the first to falter?

During a pause, Mary glanced over. "Nice shoes," she whispered.

Ruth-Ann beamed.

Mary leaned close. "Mama always gives our old stuff to the church, to help them as can't afford nice things. She gave 'em my patent leather shoes, 'cause they were scratched up. And, anyway, I have a new pair."

Ruth-Ann stared her feet. Her eyes burned. She wished she had on anything but these shiny cast-offs. Her mouth drew down in a tight-lipped grimace as she blinked back hot tears.

"Alright, children, final round." Principal Hardisty showered the room-full of sweaty captives with his myopic smile and eased his starched collar. He sounded as if he'd be as pleased as Ruth-Ann to see the end of the contest.

Ruth-Ann ground her teeth and forced her brain to concentrate.

The words came fast and furious now, as if the entire dictionary had been upended on them.

And then it happened.

Mary McConnell, scourge of the fourth-grade, missed her word. After asking for the definition and its use in a sentence, she stammered, stuttered, and stalled dead.

If Ruth-Ann could steal this word...

Ruth-Ann squeezed her eyes shut but she felt, boring into her, the steely gaze of every person in the silent classroom.

A faint, buzz caught her ear. She opened one eye and peeked at the window where a fat, fuzzy bee bumped against the glass. It wandered along the sill, and then zipped away, straight for the wild-rose bushes clustered beside the schoolyard fence.

Ruth-Ann remembered another bee, bumbling over a slim, red school-book. *Yes, there it was --- the word. She could see it on the page, plain as day.* A smile broke over her face, bright as sunrise on a summer day.

• • •

She was still grinning when she arrived home, triumphant, a blue silk rosette clutched in her sweaty fingers.

"Grade Four Champion. Oh, Sissy, I'm *that* proud of you." Ruth-Ann's mama gave her a fierce hug, then pushed her towards the stairs. "Go wash up, now. Supper's about ready. An' take them shoes off. Keep 'em nice for school."

Ruth-Ann polished the dusty patent-leather 'til it sparkled. She fingered the tiny scratch on the toe-cap, then lined up the shoes, proud and straight beside her bed, ready for the next day.

Satisfied, she leaned her elbows on the window sill and gazed at the garden.

Fat bumbles zoomed around her mama's flower beds, small, fuzzy pirates plundering the bright depths for sweet nectar and pollen, shaking the bluebells 'til they rumbled and hummed.

Ruth-Ann wasn't certain which of them had come to her aid but she knew without a doubt, one surely had.

As she scooted downstairs before her mama could start hollerin' for her, a sudden notion struck her right on the funny bone. Her nemesis, the mighty Mary McConnell, had been dethroned by a lowly 'inseck' --- a fat, fuzzy bumblebee.

No, not a bumblebee.

Ruth-Ann laughed.

A spelling bee.

• • •

The Bott's Creek Bigfoot

Run along home, Bobby,
you're too little to play with us

Always running everywhere--- that's how I remember Bobby Foster. A few years younger than the other boys, and a couple of steps behind. And always in a hurry to catch up Prob'ly from having to stop and tie his shoes. It's a wonder he never tripped over them long, red shoelaces. Always coming undone, they were. But he wouldn't use anything else. As if they were some kind of talisman --- Bobby's magic red shoelaces.

That afternoon, I was takin' ol' Buster to the Wilson place for a run. Buster still thought he was young enough to catch a rabbit. He'd never been fast enough, even as a pup, but it didn't stop him tryin'. And he was havin' a great day, larrupin' about, head high, ears flappin' in the breeze, tryin' to catch the scent of any passin' Mister Bunny.

I seen young Bobby racing across the pasture to catch up with his cousins, Shane and Mikey. Fishing poles and worm-can in hand, they were heading for Bott's Creek, where it wound through the woods behind the Wilson farm.

The woods weren't really much of a woods 'til you got farther into the hills. Mostly scrub-pine and a bunch of poplars, but the shade was cool and inviting on a hot, July day. And just beyond the old railway bridge, the fast-running creek widened out into one of the best fishing holes in the county.

Shane and Mikey were laughing, rushing on ahead.

Bobby stopped part way across the field. He laid his pole in the grass and hollered after them, "Wait up, you guys."

Shane yelled over his shoulder, "Keep up or go home, loser."

Mikey laughed and kept running. He was pretty much Shane's shadow. *Monkey see...* "Yeah, keep up, baby. Or run along home."

"Run along, baby." Their mocking voices floated back.

I could see the stubborn set of Bobby's chin from across the field.

"Am not a baby," he yelled.

By the time he finally straightened and took off after them, his cousins were almost out of sight in the woods, laughing, talking.

"Wait up, you guys." Bobby tripped on a snag and tumbled into a blackberry bush. The brambles caught at his clothes and snagged in his fair hair. One of the thorns tore a hole in the sleeve of his bright orange t-shirt.

"Ow, dang it." He fingered the hole. His ma would be mad. It was a new shirt.

Bobby rubbed the stinging scratches on his arms and forced his way through to the bank of the creek. He scanned upstream and down for his cousins.

Nothing.

No sound but the screech of a jay from the top of an old, scrub-pine.

The boys' poles were abandoned in the gravel, worm-can beside them as if it had been flung down in haste, their prized red-wrigglers scattered, writhing over the wet stones.

"Sean? Mikey? Hey, where are you? Sean? C'mon, stop foolin' around."

The jay screeched again and clouds rolled across the sun. A sudden gust ruffled the creek and set the poplar leaves clattering.

Bobby crunched towards the railway bridge, the smooth pebbles rolling and sliding under his sneakers. The creek swept around a huge curving bend there to swell and deepen under the bridge. It narrowed here; the banks rose steeply. Its friendly, chuckling gurgle became a throaty roar as the shadowed waters hurled themselves against the trestles. A tumble of rocks and boulders on either side was slick with spray.

"Sean? Mikey?" Bobby's shout echoed eerily from the trestles. His voice faltered, trailed off. It was dark under there, scary. "Sean? Are you here?"

Bobby turned and called back the way he'd come. "Mikey? Sean?"

He picked his way among the jumbled rocks, climbing towards the tracks.

A dark shape moved across the old trestle bridge. Bobby tilted his head back, squinting against the sunlight. He couldn't make out who it was. "Sean?"

The dark shape seemed to swell, reaching down, blotting out the sky. Bobby turned to run. And the rock he was braced against rolled under him, catapulting the boy into the swirling torrent.

• • •

When Sean and Mikey finally trailed in, their eyes widened at the solemn group in the kitchen. Their pa and the next-door neighbours were seated at the table with Sheriff Matthews. Two of his deputies lounged against the wall next to me, each packin' a flashlight and a huntin' rifle.

Their ma looked up from the stove. She was ladling soup into a couple of bowls. Then she placed the bowls and two spoons on a cloth-covered tray along with a plate of biscuits and carried it into the parlour.

Sean and Mikey's pa, Jace Carver, beckoned the boys over. "Where you been all afternoon?" His normal, soft drawl held an edge of steel.

The boys eyed each other. Sean opened his mouth. He closed it again real quick when Sherriff Matthews set his mug down with a sharp clink.

The sheriff leaned back in his chair and stuck a thumb in his belt. He looked the brothers up and down. "I'd think very hard about the next words out of my mouth if I was you."

Matthew's bass growl was known to intimidate strong men. Them two kids looked about ready to piss themselves. Or pass out. Or both.

Sean swallowed hard. "The movies," he mumbled, staring at his sneakers.

His pa rapped the table in front of Sean. "Speak up, boy. And mind who you're talkin' to."

36

Sean's head snapped up. "Sorry, Pa." He cleared his throat. "We were at the movies, sir, uh, Sheriff Matthews."

"All afternoon?" The sheriff transferred his hooded gaze to Mikey.

The boy's lower lip trembled, but he managed to husk out a reply. "Yes, sir. It was a double feature. we watched it three times... it, uh, it just let out."

"You two boys just up and left your young cousin, Bobby, alone by the creek and took off to the movies."

The boys drooped like a pair of whipped hounds.

"Look at me."

They faced the sheriff, pale and sweating, eyes huge. I'd been wrong. Not whipped dogs. Two terrified kids staring at certain death.

Matthews must have felt the same way I did. "Your ma's got supper in the parlour for you. After you've eaten, you wait there for me."

"Yes, sir, Sheriff Matthews."

"Yessir."

Sean and Mikey fled to the relative safety of the parlour. They knew they'd catch holy hell from their ma, but at least they weren't gonna die tonight.

Sheriff Matthews sighed. Looked at me. "Tell me again, please, Arliss."

I nodded and collected my thoughts. Put my mind back to that afternoon in Wilson's pasture.

• • •

It was gettin' warmer. I pulled off my ball cap and wiped my forehead. I was just about ready to call Buster in when I seen Sean an' Mikey come scootin' out of the brush above the bridge. They were runnin' crouched over, towards town, fast and quiet like they didn't want to be seen.

A minute later, Buster let out a yelp and headed into the woods. At first, I thought he'd finally scented a rabbit, but no, he was runnin' flat-out like he'd heard somethin' big. I charged after him, forgetting about the bramble thickets by the creek. By the time I got myself unhooked, Buster was long gone. Cursing under my breath, I picked the thorns outta my jeans and headed downstream towards the old trestle bridge.

I found some boy-sized sneaker prints beside the water and yelled for Bobby. It was hard to hear over the rushing water, but I caught a faint bark up ahead. "Buster? Buster --- what you chasin', you crazy hound? Buster!"

The boulders on one side of the trestles were disturbed, tumbled over, dark-side to the sun. Looked like somethin' had rolled 'em around. I scrambled up onto the tracks and spotted Buster off in the distance, running along the creek bed where it widened out again.

When I whistled, he come lopin' back, though. Seemed grateful for my company. I wondered what in hell he'd been chasin' to cause that. Buster wasn't acting like he'd scented a cougar. His hackles were flat. And there'd been no recent bear sightings. But I figured I'd head back to the truck for my rifle --- just to be on the safe side.

I told Buster, "Stay." He flopped down on the wet gravel. He was still there when I got back with my flashlight and twenty-two. But, he was happy enough to come with me, and the two of us old hunters followed the creek further into the woods.

Sometime later, I picked up tracks --- big --- nothin' I'd ever seen before. Buster sniffed 'em and set off after whatever'd made 'em. It was close on nine-thirty. The full moon gave good light for trackin', but I figured if we didn't find Bobby soon, we'd turn back. Prob'ly meet up with a search party. I was pretty sure Sheriff Matthews would've been alerted by now, and he'd have folks out lookin' for the little guy.

I was just about to call off ol' Buster and head for town when he stopped dead. There, on the trail in front of us, crouched some kind of big, shaggy beast. I slowly raised my rifle and sighted down the barrel. Those few seconds seemed to stretch out forever. Then I felt somethin' thumpin' against my leg. It was Buster's tail.

I looked down the barrel into the creature's face. Its eyes were warm brown. Intelligent. Not the eyes of a cornered animal. I lowered my rifle, set it on the ground beside me. Buster whined. His tail never stopped its slow tattoo.

The creature rose. The huge, shaggy thing topped me by a good two feet, but it just looked at me and shuffled back a bit. And there, curled up on the trail at its feet, was little Bobby Foster.

I checked the boy over. Nothing felt broken or out of place. His clothes were still damp --- from falling in the creek, I guessed. He had a bruise on his forehead but his breathing was even and regular.

"You fished him out of the creek, didn't you? Where were you taking him?"

The hairy thing shifted again, gazing at the sleeping boy. It folded its arms over its huge chest and made a rocking motion. Then it stared at me, its dark eyes bright with intention. Made a little huffing noise.

The sounds of a search party carried to us on the breeze, faint but closing. Dogs barking, men shouting Bobby's name.

I picked up the boy and nodded. "I'll take him home to his ma. You better go now. They'll be here right quick."

Then the creature did something I'll never forget. It put its massive face next to Bobby's and breathed in real deep as if takin' in the little boy smell of him. Then, it huffed and smoothed his hair.

I caught a glint of red in its fur. One of Bobby's shoelaces was wound around its huge wrist. The creature saw me staring and touched Bobby's sneaker, then the red lace on its arm. It huffed again, made a low hooting sound.

The hounds were baying closer. Buster barked. I swung round expecting to see the searchers crashing through the brush. When I looked back, the creature was gone. Vanished into the night.

"C'mon, Buster," I said. "Let's see if we can't give 'er a head start."

I fumbled my flashlight out and switched it on. I moved down the trail towards the search party, swingin' the light back and forth. "Hey --- here we are. Over here!"

. . .

"And that's when you found us."

Sheriff Matthews took a swig of coffee. "A huge, hairy beast?"

"Not a beast. A being, a creature."

"Okay, Arliss. A huge, hairy creature fished Bobby Foster out of the creek and then gave him to you." Matthews took another sip. "That about right?"

I nodded. Nobody had to tell me how foolish it sounded.

Matthews sighed and rolled his shoulders. "Well, that's a problem, Arliss. 'Cause what I don't need is a bunch of crazy-ass Bigfoot hunters chasing around my county shooting anything that moves."

The sheriff ran a hand through his greying hair. Eyed me with the look of a man chewin' a sour pickle. "The boy remember anything?"

"Nossir. When Bobby woke up on the way home, he asked me if I pulled him outta the creek."

Matthews nodded. "Alright. Everyone, listen up."

• • •

So, that's the story we all told. I pulled Bobby Foster outta the creek but then my truck wouldn't start. An' it was dark before anybody found us.

The Fosters moved away a while later, but I heard Bobby grew into a fine young man. Two tours in I-raq then came home an' married his high-school sweetheart. Got a job teachin' track. And nobody ever did come Bigfoot huntin' on Sheriff Matthews' patch.

But, one evening last fall, I was deep in the woods with a new dog, one of ol' Buster's pups.

Trainin' her up for a huntin' dog. And I come upon a cave, high up above Bott's Creek.

Whatever'd lived there was long dead. The carcass had been scavenged pretty bad. Just a few bones and some half-chewed bits of pelt. Bella took a sniff and whined deep in her throat. On a hunch, I took a closer look at the scattered bones. They were human-like but bigger'n any person I ever seen. And tangled among them was a frayed red shoelace.

I gathered up them bones and what was left of the fur, and dug a grave up above the old railway trestle. Covered the remains and pounded in a marker.

I stood there when I was done and watched the sunset flame over the hills to the west, wondering what to say. Finally, I tied the tattered red shoelace around the grave marker and said, simply, "Thank you."

Then I started down the hill in the soft twilight, Bella beside me, heading for home.

• • •

It's A Matter of Perspective

Stairs c'n carry ya higher 'n ya ever dreamed was possible or set ya down in a load a' trouble. All depends on where yer sittin'

Here's a secret about stairs.

I'm scared of 'em. Not so's I puke or nothin'. But when I start down a set a' stairs, my heart jerks, like I'm gonna fall. An' I hafta grab the railin'.

See, when I was two, I fell down the cellar stairs. Knocked me out cold.

I don't recall. In my mind, there's just a long, dark, wooden staircase, an' I can't see the bottom --- but my heart remembers – I

Anyways --- stairs. An' life.

I guess if it weren't fer them stairs, I wouldn't be here right now. Well, I'd be here, but I wouldn' be *here*, here, if ya catch my drift.

It all started las' night. The kind a' August night so hot ya can't think straight. The sheet sticks to yer ass no matter ya jus' took a cold shower, an' ya can't sleep fer wishin' ya lived anywheres but here.

I was out on the fire-escape, smokin' my last tailor-made. Didn' give much thought to the ruckus brewin' a few floors down. Lotta folk sittin' out, like me, tryin' a' catch a break from the heat.

So there I sat, sweatin', mindin' my own, thinkin' 'bout stairs.

Thing about staircases, see, is it's all a matter a' perspective --- whether yer stood at the bottom starin' up wonderin' can ya make it? Or yer on top lookin' down, amazed how far ya got.

Mebbe yer stopped on a landin' tryin' 'a figger out which way to go, 'cause stairways c'n branch off one way, then double back.

Ya gotta pay attention or what ya thought was a nice, smooth climb could turn inta a long slide down the other way.

See? It's really 'bout yer point a' view.-

An' from my point a' view jus' then, bein' four flights up from a yellin' match, stayin' put was prob'ly my best option. Mama didn' raise no fool.

47

Then again, mebbe she did, 'cause next minute, I'm scrapin' my ass up off the stair an' headin' down. I jus' can't abide a man smackin' his mama. No, sir.

Them rusty metal treads squealed and groaned like I was my fat Aunt Mabel, creakin' down ta the bathroom at three in the a.m., but them two was so busy scrappin' neither one heard me comin'.

From wheres I stood, the ol' lady was givin' as good as she got. Still –

"Hey! Mick!" I had to holler twice ta get his attention. "Y'oughtta be ashamed."

Mick stopped mid-slap an' stared. So, did his mama.

Mick --- Michelangelo Alfonso De La Torre --- usually went by Mickey Towers, or Tall Mickey. Made-man. Real up-'n'-comer. Right now he was piss-drunk an' mean as a stepped-on dock rat. The four-legged kind. An' faster'n a snake with that switchblade he carried in his back pocket.

His mama cussed him out in I-talian an' smacked him upside the head with her wooden pasta roller. It staggered Mick some, but didn' put 'im down.

She hauled off fer another shot, but Mick wasn' havin' it. He swore an' grabbed her arm. Shoved the ol' lady inta the railin'.

I lunged past 'im an' made a grab for Missus Towers an' yanked her back

Heard Mick scream -- it cut off sharp.

I stared over the railin' at Mick's brains splashed across the alley, three floors below. I musta knocked him over when I caught his mama, an' it looked like he'd hit his head on his way down.

She tried to pull away.

"No, don't look, Missus. Don't go down."

No power this side a' heaven coulda stopped her. She raced down them three flights a' stairs like they was nothin' an' fell on her knees beside Mick.

"No, mio Dio, no. Aiee! Figlio mio, figlio mio. Hai ucciso mio figlio. Ti strapperò il cuore. Ho maledetto la tua anima all'inferno."

That's *'Ya killed my son. I'm gonna rip out yer heart. Burn in Hell.'* More 'r less.

She was still wailin' fer blood when the cops showed up an' dragged me away.

Down at the station house, the wide cop across from me pickin' his teeth thought the whole thing was hi-larious. He couldn' stop laughin'.

"Bert, shut up an' lemme think, fer Pete's sake." The tall, thin cop fired up a tailor-made an' offered the pack.

I don' usually smoke with cops, but under the circumstances – besides, they was tailor-mades.

"Seems you ain't exac'ly Mr. Popularity right now, Artie, what with helpin' Mickey Towers down the stairs." *Funny man.*

Oh, Artie? That's me ---Arthur Poe, twen'y-three, one-time gofer fer Mickey Towers. Current job prospeck's, very poor.

"But, in all fairness, kid, ya done us a big favor."

News to me. "How so?"

"Your boss, well, your ex-boss, was becoming a real nuisance. But you just solved that little problem for us, so we're gonna reciprocate." He cocked an eyebrow. "Ya know what that means, kid? Reciprocity?"

"Ya mean 'tit-fer-tat,' right? Yeah, Mick's guys're pretty big on that. I figger there's a big 'tat' comin' my way."

Thin cop parked his butt on a corner of the table. "I'm gonna help ya out, kid. One time offer. A bus ticket outta here. Whaddya say?"

What could I say? "Uh, thanks."

He didn' waste no time. The desk sergeant signed his chit for petty cash. Then thin cop led me down the narrow, cement back-stairs outa the cop-shop, an' whisked me off to the bus station.

He tol' me his name --- Detective Malloy. All the way to the depot, he kep' yakkin' about 'The Rules': I could never come back, I hadda change my name, lay low, stay outta trouble, an' a pile a' other stuff.

When we got there, he pointed at the nearest bus. The sign beside it read, "Billings, Big Timber, Three Forks, Butte, Helena, Townsend, White Sulfur Springs"

I snickered. "Where's 'Butt'?"

"It's 'Bee-yoot' An' it's in Montana?"

"Great." *Didn' sound great.* "Where's Montana?"

Malloy handed me a ticket. "Where you're goin'."

I shrugged. "So, what's in Montana?"

"Cows. Trees. Snow. No gangsters. You'll like it."

Yeah, sure. Dang stairs still weren't done messin' with my life.

I clambered up them three metal steps onto that fancy Greyhound Silversides, an' plunked my ass in the first empty spot.

"Excuse me, is that seat taken?"

I stared, pinned by a pair a' beautiful grey eyes. "*Like sunlight dancing on a clear mountain stream.*" Mama had read me that outta one a' her ladies' romance magazines. Back then, it sounded kinda sappy, but starin' into them dazzlers, I figgered that writer fella hit it dead on.

"No ma'am." I jumped up so's she could have the winda' seat. Mama woulda been proud. Nearly tripped over my feet tryin' 'a be a gentleman.

Once we was settled, she stuck out her hand. "Alice Pennybaker."

Detective Malloy's warnin' rang in my ears, *'Whatever you do, Artie, don't use your real name again. Ever.'* "Uh, Roy... Roy... Bennet?"

She smiled. "You don't sound too sure, Roy."

Sweat slid down my armpits, threatenin' to swamp my five-day deodorant. I cleared my throat an' tried not ta sound like a kid on his first date. "No'm, it's Roy Bennet."

Alice gazed at me with them bright eyes. It felt rude not sayin' anythin' else. "I'm headin' fer Montana, fer work."

An' there went Rule #2 --- 'Never volunteer information. Only tell 'em what they ask, an' only if ya hafta.' Malloy had been real clear on that one, too.

She had a nice smile --- friendly, nice white teeth. "So am I. I'm moving back home to Helena."

"Helena sounds nice."

She nodded. "Lived there most of my life. I can show you 'round if you'd like."

Things were lookin' up.

But, see, that's what I mean about stairs. Here I am, a guy from the city goin' nowheres fast, an' now I'm sittin' beside Miss Alice Pennybaker on a shiny new bus, headed for Helena, Montana.

It's all a matter a' perspective.

• • •

A Dog An' His Boy

Never mess with a dog's best friend

First time I set eyes on the kid I knowed he was trouble. Skinny four-foot-nothin' in ripped jeans an' a stained t-shirt. All elbows an' knees an' a stick-straight, dark-brown hair. Goofy-lookin' yella' pup trailin' after 'im. One part pit-bull, three parts anybody's-guess. It larruped down the alleyway trippin' over too-big paws, somethin' danglin' from its drooly mouth. Stub of a tail waggin' fer the pure joy a' runnin' with his boy.

They charged past me outta the shadowed alleyway an' up the sun-scorched street. Screen door banged, where the kid an' his mutt squirted out from.

"Take this one, too, ya dumb shit."

A ratty sneaker come whizzin' outta the gloom. Landed with a thump near where I was sittin' on my back stoop. Whoever'd flung it had a pretty fair arm. The whiskey-soaked voice shouted again an' the door slammed shut. From the sounds of it, the kid 'ud be smart to stay away fer a while.

I seen 'em round 'most ever' day after that. Crazy mutt flyin' down the street behind his boy, somethin' in his mouth. A slipper, a beat-up loafer. One time, it was draggin' an ol' rubber boot. Then they wasn't around fer a while.

I confess to bein' a mite curious. Not about sneaker-man. I know a mean drunk when I hear one. 'Sides, his kind don't end up here fer bein' upstandin' citizens.

Ever' city spawns a place like this, then tries t' ignore it. Fulla stuff folks got no more use fer. So, the city shits it out, an it oozes downhill 'til it lands here.

Our partic'lar patch a' desperation used to be a lonely stretch a' tidal flats. Wild grass an' water birds. Couple a' big ol' houses on the river's edge. Skiffs tied up to a crumbling stone jetty. Sometimes you'd see a blue egret stalkin' through the shallows, spear-fishin' fer frogs. At low tide, them flats was treacherous. The road

56

cuttin' 'crost it socked in solid damn near ever'
night. Wall a' fog so thick yer head-lights
bounced right off it. In winter, the pavement was
slick as a friggin' skatin' rink.

All gone now. Smothered by cracker-box
row-houses an' shit-hole, low-rise apartments.
Few mom-n-pop stores fightin' to stay afloat.
Rubbin' shoulders with pawn shops an' peep-
shows. An' bars, a' course. But, the fog still rolls in
thick off the river most nights. Softens the hard
edges. Makes ya think a' ghosts and such.

Lookin' back now, I remember I didn' waste
much thought on sneaker-man. I had his
number. But I wondered about the youngster an'
his yella' dog.

Next time I seen 'em, I was nursin' a beer at
Dusty's. A hole-in-the-wall with a half-dozen
tables an' a battered, stand-up bar down one
side. Dusty ain't his real name. But Dusty says
nobody 'ud trust a bar-keep named Ignatius.
Me, I wouldn' trust him anyways. His name got
nuthin' to do with it. A peelin' sign in the fly-
specked front window reads 'Dusty's Saloon ---

Lager on Tap.' Ever'body as drinks here knows Dusty waters his booze. Can't fault him too much fer that. Jus' business. But to call the horse-piss he has on tap 'Lager' is purely sinful. Can't trust a man 'ud sell this shit an' call it Lager.

But, there was the kid in the doorway, a string looped through the yella' mutt's collar. Poised, wary. Eyes dartin' around. I knowed that look. He was checkin' fer somebody an' hopin' they wasn't here.

Dusty hollered from the back. "Git. An' take that mangy mutt with ya."

"Please, mister. This one a' Dan's dogs. Dan say he stop by later an' square up if you give us lunch."

One a' Dan's dogs. Now, it was startin' to make sense. Dan was Mick Donovan's new trainer. S'posed to have some big-time connections. Help Mick get a leg up. But the kid was young to be one a' Dan's helpers.

Dusty eye-balled the boy. "Don't run no tabs. Not even fer Dan."

Kid shrugged. "Jus' doin' what he say, mister. I'll tell him you didn' wanna" He turned to go.

Dusty blanched. "Wait up, there. I'll feed ya." He headed fer the kitchen in back a' the bar. "But, I ain't feedin' no damn dog," he muttered.

The kid looked around, uncertain. I waved him over an' pulled out a chair.

The youngster perched on the edge a' the seat, hangin' on tight to his string. He'd growed some since I seen 'im last. So'd the pup. It sniffed my pant legs an' drooled over my shoes. Kid give the string a tug an' the mutt settled at his feet, bony head restin' on the boy's sneakers.

"So, you're one a Dan's boys," I said.

Kid flinched. "You know Dan?"

I shook my head. "Know of him. He works fer my boss." Mick Donovan ran other things 'sides dog fights. Numbers. Loans. I was one a' his collectors. I leaned back an' took another sip. Grimaced as the lukewarm brew hit the few a' my taste-buds as still worked. "How long you been with Dan?"

"Few months." Kid was watchin' me out the corner of his eye. Tryin' a figger should he run 'er stay put. "He sprung me from a crap foster home. Tol' 'em he's my uncle."

He clammed up when Dusty hustled over with his burger an' fries. Dusty banged the plate down and retreated behind the bar. Them fries was plenty dark. Stunk a' cookin' oil on the turn. Starvin' wolves woulda passed 'em by, but the kid tucked right in. Between bites, his hand 'ud slide under the table with a chunk a' burger.

I waited. After a bit, he started talkin' again. "I help him with the pups, mostly."

I nodded. The dog's moist nose snuffled my ankle. Gentle teeth nibbled my laces. I moved my foot out a' range. "What's his thing with shoes?"

Kid shrugged. "Dunno. He don' chew 'em. He jus' love ta carry 'em around." A mischievous grin lit the boy's grubby face. "Course, he don' much like ta give 'em back."

"Ever get him a proper dog toy?"

Kid shook his head. "He jus' like shoes."

A shadow fell 'crost our table. A calloused hand shot out an' smacked the kid upside the head. Almos' knocked him offa the chair. *Damn. I hadn't been payin' proper attention. Sneaker-man had snuck up on us, large as life an' twice as ugly.*

"Tol' ya' to clean them dog pens, not feed yer face." Dan grabbed the kid by the collar an' shook 'im.

I pushed my chair back an' stood up slow. Like I said, I'm one a' Mick's collectors. I figger it's only fair to give a man a chance to think on what he's dealin' with.

Dan craned 'is neck to take in my hefty six-foot-five. His eyes bugged out an' he stopped shakin' the kid. Gotta give 'im credit, though. He never let go. He dragged the pair outside an' glared at Dusty from the safety a' the doorway. Pointed at the kid's empty plate. "I ain't payin' fer that." Then they was gone.

I threw a ten-spot on the table. Walked over to the window an' stared after 'em.

Dusty frowned an' fingered the bill. Decided he'd best not ask fer a tip. "You want 'nother beer?"

"Nah, think I'm gonna take in the fights."

His mouth opened, then he squinted at me. Shut his teeth over whatever else he was gonna say, an' retreated, hands fulla dirty dishes.

It was dark by the time I made it to Mick's warehouse. Few a' Mick's boys was standin' roun' shootin' the shit. Fight ring was empty --- a shoulder-high, steel-mesh box with corner-posts sunk in cement, an' a low, dog-door at each end. The locked room where they kep' the dogs had a double row a' pens on three walls. The fourth held shelves fulla food an' vet supplies. Kinda like a animal shelter. Only not.

Crash. The door to the dog room banged open an' Dan stormed out wavin' a man's Oxford. Had the kid by one arm. The yella' pup' teeth was locked on a mouthful a' Dan's trouser leg.

Kid was screamin', "Lemme go. Lemme go. Don' you touch my dog."

"You little shit, I'll show you what happens when you don' do what I tell ya." Dan tossed the Oxford inta the ring. Dog let go the pantleg an' flung hisself after the shoe. Circlin' the ring fer a way in. Dan dragged the kid back inta the dog room. There was a bunch a' rattlin' an' clangin'. Lotta cussin'. Mick's guys an' me glanced at each other, wonderin' what was next.

Then it all went to shit. The dog-room door slammed back on its hinges. Dan come flyin' out, surrounded by a pack a' snarlin', four-footed combatants. Night was fulla shouts, an' screams, an' yelpin' dogs. One a' Mick's guys started shootin'.

I spotted the kid in the melee. Hoisted 'im inta the ring. "Stay there. I'll find yer mutt."

Then, fast as the fight started, it was done.

Cops busted through the overhead doors. Rolled in sirens blarin', with a couple S.P.C.A. vans. Fog rolled in with 'em. Uniforms yellin' an' swearin', roundin' up dogs an' stuffin' 'em in vans. Mick's guys yellin' an' swearin', gettin' shoved in the back a' cop cars. Red lights strobin'. Evr'thin' swirlin' in an' outta the mist in a crazy ghost-dance.

I found the yella' pup layin' beside one a' the pens. He'd been booted in the head an' one eye was swole shut, but his teeth was locked tight on Dan's shoe. No trace a' Dan. I scooped up the mutt, grabbed the kid outa the ring, an' headed fer Dusty's 'fore them uniforms set their sights on us. Jus' got 'em cleaned up when Mick sauntered in with a couple a' goons. He spotted us right off.

"Been a busy night," he said. "Cops busted up my warehouse. Scooped my dogs. Trainer's in the wind. I gotta wonder how that happened."

I kep' my face blank. I didn't hafta wonder --- kid tol' me he opened them cages an' called the cops.

Mick didn't really expect an answer. He's a pretty good guesser. He pointed at the yella' mutt crouched at my feet. "All but that one."

The pup growled deep in his throat. He raised his head up off the boy's sneakers. His good eye fixed on Mick's shoes.

Mick looked at me 'n' did the math. "Fair enough. I know when ta cut my losses." He settled his jacket. "Anythin' we need to discuss?"

I shook my head 'no'.

"Then I see no need fer this to go any further? D' you?"

I shook my head again.

"Them two're your look-out, now. Best keep 'em outta my sight."

I nodded. Mick an' his goon's left. I took a sip a' beer. I sure hoped Mick was tellin' it straight. That he'd leave 'em alone.

Ju's to be safe, though, I'm gonna send 'em upstate to my sister. Her 'n' Ernie got a big farm there. An' they like kids. Hope they like dogs. I figger the kid c'n teach that yella' hound to herd chickens. Now, that 'ud be somethin' to see. Who knows, mebbe the crazy mutt'll give up shoes fer a feathered dog-toy.

• • •

The Ark

When the waters rise will we return to "that time?"

To what we were before we crawled from below?

"Is this what happens when the world cries?"

We ask and yet no answer have...

Up, to breathe the crystal air,

We rose, and rising, changed;

And now, must return —

With the fishes,

Shall we

Sleep?

Shall we

Ever rise again?

Walk earth, breathe air,

Become what once we were?

From deep inside the questions rise,

"What have we learned, to try again?"

For rise we must, endure we must, and build,

And strive to have, to hold, to live;

We do not own, but are —

Owned of the earth;

Once beloved,

Now below

We lie…

Is this what happens when the world cries?

. . .

"Is the world crying, Daddy?"

Aaron stared through fly-specked glass at the grey, foggy drizzle. Ninety days straight, they hadn't seen the sun. The damn fog had followed them from San Francisco. Nevada was supposed to be hot. Sunny. *A desert, for God's sake.*

They'd moved inland after Sam's mother died. Aaron had always hated winter at the coast. Freezing rain. Ice-rimed streets.

But, since the change, it was the same everywhere. Aaron's head felt as if it was stuffed with cotton wool. He was never dry or warm. The bed-sheets were cold and clammy when he crawled in at night.

"Is it?"

His son's words finally penetrated the mist clogging his brain.

Aaron shook his head to clear it. "Is it what?"

"Is the world crying?"

Aaron stared. "What are you talking about, Sam?"

"Grandpa says the rain is God's tears. But, Auntie Ruth says it's the world crying for help."

Sammy'd been only a year old when they were forced higher into the mountains to escape the rising water. So many drowned cities. So many homeless. Hard-scrabble settlements bloomed like cancerous lesions --- miles of cardboard shelters and tent-ghettos strung out along every major roadway.

They'd been lucky to find this abandoned trapper's cabin. Its weathered logs stunk of long-dead animal --- the crumbling pelts Ruth and Aaron dragged outside and burned when they first arrived. At least, the roof didn't leak.

"I don't know, Sam..." His voice trailed off. *How d'you explain severe climate change to a five-year-old?* Aaron wasn't sure he truly grasped the magnitude of it himself.

Governments, the military, big multi-nationals, everyone'd had a hand in trying to slow it down, to reverse the damage. They'd stopped the converter program --- shut down the network of mighty, ocean-cooled condensers which harnessed the sun's energy.

The condensers were supposed to be a boon, to save humanity. They were designed to replace polluting fossil fuels and save their power-starved world. And the program had worked, at first. But, something went wrong. What was left of the ice caps melted. Sea-levels rose catastrophically submerging the low-lying, coastal areas.

Then, the rains came. The massive influx of fresh water diluted the oceans and further destabilized the system. Even after the converters were taken off-line, the flooding continued.

Many, like Sammy's grandfather, believed their world was finally cleansing itself, perhaps to begin again. Some of the *enders* as they were called, pitched their tents in the foot-hills to prepare for the final coming with prayer and celebration. Their old-fashioned hymns about "goin' to glory" and the "better world awaitin'," echoed through the mountain passes.

Some banded together in tight, well-armed communities. They stockpiled supplies and collected whatever or whoever they decided should be saved. They took what they needed, by force, if necessary. And built huge arks, massive ships to bear them safely above the coming flood.

Aaron knew of an ender group, close by.

He gazed at his son --- so like his mother, with her dark curls and sparkling hazel eyes. The boy was tall for his age, and smart. Sammy already knew how to read and write. He loved animals. Even the wild ones would take food from his hand. Maybe, if Aaron was lucky –

"C'mon, Sam. We have to pack." Aaron grabbed the boy's shoulder and pushed him towards the bedroom. He yanked open drawers, stuffing Sam's clothes into a carry-sack.

"What about Grandpa and Auntie Ruth? Should they pack, too?" Sam stroked the ears of a black cat curled in the middle of his pillow. She yawned and stretched, purred at the boy's touch and offered her swollen belly for a rub.

"They'll be fine. They'll understand."

"We'll understand what?"

Aaron spun around. His father and sister watched from the doorway. "We'll understand what?" his father repeated.

"I'm sorry, Dad, Ruthie --- but, I have to try. Please. It may be our only chance."

"You're not taking the boy to those *enders*. He belongs with his family." Aaron's father reached for the boy. "Come here, Samuel."

Before Sammy could move, Ruth touched her father's outstretched arm. "No, Dad, Aaron's right. We have to save Sam."

"Save me from what?" Sammy pressed close to his father.

Aaron knelt by the boy. "You have to be brave, Sam. Can you do that for me?"

Wide-eyed, the boy nodded.

"Good. Let's finish packing. We have to hurry."

With the help of Aaron's father and sister, Sam's clothes, some warm, heavy blankets and all their provisions were stuffed in kit-bags and stowed in their SUV. Aaron held out a hand for Sam's carry-all as he bundled the boy into the back seat.

The boy wrapped both arms round the unwieldy pack. "No, Dad. It's okay."

Driving rain turned the rough track up the mountain into a slippery, rutted quagmire. No-one spoke. It was too hard to be heard over the rising wind and the rhythmic, frantic slapping of the over-taxed wipers, as they strained to keep up with the deluge.

Thunder crashed and growled overhead. Blinding, sulfurous flares streaked across the skies as the storm clawed the plateau like a ravening beast. Muddy cataracts uprooted trees and gouged chunks from the road.

At last, the SUV crested a rise and slid onto the high plateau. Aaron braked hard and stared at the armed men who barred the gates to the compound.

"Please, I need to speak to whoever's in charge."

A burly, dark-bearded man raised his rifle. "You c'n speak to us."

Aaron climbed out and pulled Sam forward. He gestured for Ruth and their father to get out. "Please, take us with you. We have extra food, blankets. Some tools."

The man shook his head. "No room."

"Then, take my son and my sister. Please. I beg you, take them with you."

Another man stepped forward, rifle at the ready. "Leave the packs and go."

"Enough."

A tall, grizzled man strode from the shadows by the gate into the twin cones of light from the SUV's headlamps. He pushed back his hood and brushed long strands of wind-whipped, graying hair out of his dark eyes. "I'm sorry, but Cain's right, we have no room."

Aaron pushed Sam into the light. The little boy shivered in the steady downpour, clutching his carry-all. "He's a good boy. A hard worker. My sister's a medic. Please." Aaron's voice broke. Numb, frozen, he sank to his knees in the mud.

The tall man shook his head. "I'm sorry. You'd best go --- get out of the storm."

Aaron studied the tall man's exhausted face and red-rimmed eyes, dark with strain and loss. "There's nowhere left to go."

He struggled to his feet and helped his father into their vehicle. Carefully buckled him in. Then he unloaded their bags and bales and piled them beside his sister. He hugged Ruth, and kissed her on both cheeks, shouting above the wind, "Take care of Sam."

He picked up his son. Holding fast to his carry-all, the boy tucked his head into Aaron's neck. "Mind your Auntie Ruth. And, always remember, I'm very proud of you. I love you, Sam."

The little boy nodded.

Aaron placed the boy and his bundle in Ruth's arms, and turned towards the armed men. "There really is nowhere to go."

He walked to the SUV and slid inside, quickly reversing down the road. At the first bend, he cranked the vehicle around and cut the lights. They raced down the narrow, bumpy track in the dark, checking behind for any sign they'd been followed.

"They'll be alright, Dad. He won't leave them."

"How can you be sure?"

"He has kind eyes, Dad. He still cares. He won't leave them." Aaron smiled at his father. Neither man saw the towering wall of seething, dark water bearing down on them out of the heart of the storm.

• • •

A gleaming, brass ship's lantern over the cabin's only bunk swayed on its gimbals in time with the rhythmic creaking of the ark. The tall man stooped in doorway of the tiny, low-ceilinged cabin, haloed in the flickering glow. He eyed the little boy sleeping in his auntie's arms.

It had been a long night. His people barely made it into the arks before mountainous waves washed away every trace of their settlement. One of the ships foundered, unable to close its huge bow-doors in time --- twelve people and untold species lost. He and his son had managed to save a few of the animals, but now their own ark was dangerously overcrowded. And, no telling how long they'd be adrift, or what would be left if and when the waters abated.

And these newcomers? He knew they'd been placed in his hands for a reason --- sent to him. So, whatever else might be in store, they were his to care for, now.

The boy's carry-sack wriggled. A muffled "mrrow" issued from its depths.

The tall man set the bag on the bunk and untied the fasteners. A black cat poked her head out. Spotting Sam, she made her way across the blankets and curled up in the boy's lap.

The man ran a large hand across his face and scrubbed away a smile. His eyes twinkled. "A pregnant cat."

The woman's lips quirked. "She'll keep the mice down. And her kittens will be a welcome diversion."

"Your brother knew I'd take you."

She nodded. "Aaron is --- was --- a good judge of character. My name is Ruth, by the way. And you are?"

The man offered his hand. "Pleased to meet you, Ruth. I'm called Noah."

• • •

The Last Voyage of Compass Rose

The story of the lost ark

Alone in her corner, the old woman crouched on a thread-bare pallet and clutched her sole possession, an ancient compass. The lifeless needle once pointed north, strong and true, showing the way home --- so, she'd been told.

Her mother's mother had given her the compass, passed down from eldest daughter to eldest daughter, always named Rose, like her mother before her. Each new Compass Rose would look to the heavens and use her north-pointing needle to guide the clan across the dark waters.

The stars had always been the old woman's friends --- a book she read with ease. But she'd borne only sons. Her sons wed and spawned sons as well, and their sons, sons. Now she was old and alone, with no daughter of her loins or of her line to carry on her legacy, for none of her sons' wives or grandsons' wives could tell one point of light from another.

Old and infirm, with failing eye-sight, the old woman could no longer scan the night sky to read the stars. She was consigned to the scrap-heap of useless passengers, begrudged her morning bowl of watered-gruel with its sop of bread. Meat rarely found its way onto her evening plate of mashed greens.

Most days, she sat alone on her pallet and dreamed of life 'before' --- before the deluge drowned their world and drove them onto the arks, where they floated at the mercy of the waves.

Ark Six was one of seven vessels remaining from the original ten. At first, everyone aboard her prayed for the waters to recede and let them walk on dry land once more. Now, they prayed for little and hoped for less, except to see another day. Sometimes, not even that. When the snows came and winter storms raged, most prayed only for release.

But, the old woman still hoped. And dreamed. Her mind was filled with friends --- Baby Bird, whose shimmering wings of blue and green had carried her to a kinder place; Cat-man-do, who'd crossed over many years ago, but whose soft fur and purring voice lingered like a warm scarf round chilly shoulders; General Dog's-body, the last of his kind. Fierce and loyal to the end, he'd given his life protecting her.

As she retreated from reality, the people around her took on the affects of her inner world. Her quick-footed grandson growled and thundered, shaggy-maned, about his lair. He tore his food with sharp, white teeth, a Lion Man. His mate, Mouse Woman, shivered and cowered. Lion Man's slightest roar sent her a-scurry to avoid his hard-fisted anger. Their sons, the Monkey Boys, screeched and scratched, and fought each other for the choicest fruit and the softest resting place.

But one was different, a disappointment to his father's father and therefore to his clan. Oh, he ran rough-and-tumble with the rest, but he saw faces in the clouds and danced in the rain to music he alone heard.

He sat with the old woman and listened to her stories. He dreamed with her of a place where the sun shone on their faces as they wandered through fields of wild clover, and in return, the old woman showed him the stars.

"Look there. Those five bright ones make a "W" --- the old woman in a chair."

The boy laughed. "Like you, Granny?"

"Like me." Her faded, grey eyes twinkled. The wrinkles etched 'round them from years of gazing at the heavens deepened. "There --- the Swan, the Water Bearer, the Southern Cross -- now, you show me. Tell me their names."

So, he did, and so, again, until he knew them well as his own.

They found an iron nail, wrapped it in a bit of copper wire and bound it to the mast to catch lightning from a storm. Then she showed him how to stroke it on the pointed needle of her compass 'til it swung towards North again.

She taught him the cardinal directions, and how to read the four winds and understand the markings on the old charts.

"This is a – a reef?"

The corners of the old woman's mouth lifted. "Or a shoal, yes. And, see here? This is the mark for a channel, between those islands."

"What's an island, Granny?"

And then, one night, it ended. The clan decided to scuttle the ark.

Lion Man roared and shook his mane. "We've been cursed. The land will never rise again. Better to give up now than keep on 'til we're all mad like the crazy fools in the other arks who still believe."

Mouse Woman wept and clung to her babies, though they were much too big to hide behind her skirts.

The old woman clutched her compass and faded into her mind.

The boy crept to her pallet that night. "Granny, what can we do."

He shook her shoulder. She didn't move. He pried the compass from her match-stick fingers and held it before her face. "Look, Granny. it still points north."

The old woman opened her eyes and sighed. "You must gather all the food you can carry, and water-skins. Hide them behind my pallet. No-one will bother with an old woman. When it's dark, steal a raft and sail to another ark. One of them will surely take you in 'til the land rises again."

The boy crept away and the next day, he brought food and water.

She was right. No-one paid any mind to a disappointing boy and a worthless old woman. They were all too busy preparing their last supper --- a feast. No more stinting or saving. No holding back, now.

When the moon rose that night, the clan gathered below-deck, everyone in their best. Everyone ate too much, then purged and gorged themselves again. Most drank 'til they were drunk. They danced and sang. Man and maid alike lay with any who pleased their eye, willing or no. Shouts and screams rent the blood-red night, but there was no mercy save the kiss of a sharp blade.

When all was still, the old woman and the boy crept out of hiding. She tried to make him leave her, but in the end, he proved more stubborn than she, so, both fled the silent, sinking ark.

• • •

Day after endless, scorching day, the boy held the tiller and guided their raft northward. The old woman consulted the compass and kept their course true. The winds held fair and filled their single sail.

Then the winds died. Their food low, their water near an end, the boy sat with the old woman in the shade of their canvas sail.

She told him about life 'before' --- the little she remembered and the stories of her mother's mother. He marveled at the idea of a cat as sleek and fast and large as the one she called a cheetah, and the huge, grey animal with flapping ears, wrinkled legs, and a writhing snout that sprayed water. He laughed 'til tears came when she trumpeted loud, squealing, fart-like noises.

"An elephant? There never was such a thing." He held his stomach and slapped their sleeping mat as she squeaked and squalled. "Ow, stop."

The old woman laughed, too, a creaky rasp, rusty from long disuse. "No, I promise. It was as real as I am."

"I don't believe you. You made it up."

As the days wore on, they talked less. They slept while the sun blazed. At night, the boy steered by the stars and prodded the old woman awake to check her compass.

"Keep going." Her faint whisper rasped through cracked lips.

The boy nodded.

One night, she wouldn't waken. He tried shaking her but finally lay down beside her. "I'm not giving up, Granny. I promise. I'll just sleep here with you for a while."

He dozed through that night and long into the next. Sometime after moon-rise, a sudden lurch jolted him awake. He stared up into the soft glow of a ship's lantern.

"Hey, boy! You on the raft. You alive?"

The boy scrambled to his feet. "I'm alive. We're alive. Throw us a rope." He bent to the old woman. "Granny, we made it. We found another ark."

"Look out, there." A burly man shinned down the rope. He gazed at the motionless woman and the boy kneeling beside her.

Tears rolled down the boy's cheeks. "Her name was Rose. She taught me to read the stars."

He took the battered compass from the old woman's lifeless hand. "She said this would always bring me home."

The old woman smiled down from the night sky. She was already home.

• • •

Home is the Sailor

From the ink-dark deeps, we will rise again

Jem leaned against the heavy oak stanchion, sturdy, sun-browned legs braced against the heavy rolling of the ark.

"D'ya see 'em yet, Jem?" Saree grabbed her brother's arm and leaned as far over the railing as she could stretch her nine-year-old frame. Her other hand shaded her eyes from the fierce reflected glare of the sun.

Saree's curls were as dark as Jem's were fair, and she was as outspoken as Jem was quiet. Their mam said whatever popped into Saree's mind came right out her mouth.

"Shouldn't they be here by now, the other arks? At least one of 'em?"

"They'll be here. It's early days yet. Give 'em time, Saree."

Saree sank back with a sigh and clutched the small, leather pouch dangling from a braided thong under her shirt. The well-worn leather was soft, silky to the touch, and the sweet scent of the teaspoon or so of earth it contained drifted up, warm from her body. Every arker carried a similar talisman --- a reminder of the home they'd lost.

The vessel creaked and groaned as it shouldered into the choppy seas. There was no cross-wind to speak of, beyond a light breeze, so Jem reckoned they must be nearing shallow waters to slosh around so much. Most days their huge craft skimmed the waves light as a child's toy instead of the unwieldy, multi-ton behemoth it was. But, it had carried their families safely above the stormy deeps for generations.

Jem and Saree's home-ark was one of seven, now. Ark Ten foundered and sank in the first of the world-drowning storms.

Since then, two more had been lost.

Ark Nine was claimed by the northern seas. Her captain hit a long stretch of shallows and thought he'd found a place where the old shore-line was rising. In his rush to find land, he tore the bottom out of his ark on a fathoms-deep, jagged tangle of long-dead trees and twisted metal.

A few made it into the life rafts. Their desiccated remains were found months later, along with a journal.

Whoever'd kept it had been strong. Strong enough to survive for weeks in an open boat on nothing but rain-water and hope. Those few, scribbled pages, read aloud every *Gathering*, were some of the strangest, saddest, and yet, most beautiful words Jem had ever heard in all his eleven years.

After Ark Nine's tragic end, Jem's people shunned the shallows, wary of what lay hidden below. The old charts couldn't be trusted. Shorelines had shifted. Wreckage from the old-timers' drowned cities clogged the sea-lanes.

Ark Six simply vanished. It had sailed away from a Gathering and never returned.

The remaining arks roamed the seething waves, nomads searching for signs of Rising --- the hoped-for days when the oceans would recede and the water-borne would walk on dry land once more.

Every warm season, when their world hung closest to its sun and the cold rains withdrew to the north, the arks made their way together. Seedlings and animals were traded, children fostered to their sister arks to keep the gene-pool strong, unions celebrated, losses mourned.

Old-timer stories were told; stories of the earth-born, chronicles of their life before The Flood. New chapters were added; stories of the water-born. Songs were sung. And every Gathering ended with the same poem --- a prayer now, recited by one of the elders.

This year would be the turn of Jem's great-grandpa, Samuel, the last of the earth-born.

Under the wide and starry sky,
Dig the grave and let me lie.
Glad did I live and gladly die,
And I laid me down with a will
This be the verse you grave for me:
'Here he lies where he longed to be;
Home is the sailor, home from sea,

And the hunter home from the hill.'[1]

None of the young-uns, Jem included, had ever seen dry land except in picture books. They had no concept of digging a grave or burial --- not in the way the poem meant. The only grave they knew was the dark water below, where the shroud-wrapped dead were sent to their rest.

Oh, the children understood digging and planting. Every ark held its own cubit of earth, apart from the hydroponics which provided food for every creature on-board. The earth resided in a huge, sturdy, metal-lined box where a few, special seedlings were cherished.

The young-uns learned to care for their earth. To turn the rich compost of vegetable leavings and table scraps. To water and fertilize the crumbly, dark soil and make sure it stayed sweet. And above all, to keep track of the worms.

"Healthy worms make healthy soil," Jem's father was fond of saying.

Saree's heavy sigh dragged Jem from his thoughts. "I wish they'd get here."

A smile lifted the corners of his mouth. "You know what Mam says about wishes, don'tcha?"

Saree giggled. "If wishes were horses, the beggars would ride." She scanned the empty horizon. "Jem, d'you think we'll ever get to ride a horse?"

"Mebbe – " Jem's grey eyes searched the skies.

"Da says they have a new foal on Ark Five. Mebbe we'll get fostered there. Does bein' fostered make you a beggar, Jem? I asked Mam and she said we're all just wandering beggars, now." Saree tugged at Jem's sleeve. "What'd she mean, Jem?"

Before he could answer, a shout rang from the crow's nest, the lookout's perch high above on the main mast. "To the north --- a bird."

Jem scampered up the ladder to the cages with Saree close behind as the tired pigeon fluttered to a perch. Jem removed the message-case from its leg, his fingers swift from long practice. When he released the bird into the pen with the others, it headed straight for the seed dishes.

A small knot of arkers had gathered on the after-deck below the bird cages. Jem clambered down and offered the tiny, painted case to the burly man at the front of the group.

Deep-etched lines crinkled the weather-beaten skin 'round eyes as blue as the southern seas. White teeth flashed against his bushy, black beard. He cocked a quizzical brow at the children.

"Bird had a long flight. Who sent it?"

Saree pushed in front Jem. "Ark Four, Cap'n."

Jem pointed to the case's intricate design. "It's their colors inked on the carrier-tube, sir."

The captain prised the top from the tiny tube with his thumbnail and spilled the message-scroll into his palm. He unrolled tight-wrapped paper and read.

His head came up and he scanned the horizon for the space of a long, slow breath. Then, his hooded gaze returned to the message.

"Good new, Cap'n?"

"How fares Ark Four, sir?"

The white teeth flashed again in a smile that didn't quite reached the captain's eyes. "Ark Four fares well, very well --- they've sighted land."

Saree had been watching the captain. A puzzled frown puckered her forehead. As she opened her mouth to speak, Jem pinched her arm. Hard.

Saree rounded on him. "What'd you do that for?"

Jem pulled her aside as the men headed below decks to spread their news. "Something's wrong, Saree." He raised a hand to ward of the flood of questions he saw forming behind her eyes. "C'mon. We gotta find Da."

Smoke from the ship's lanterns hung in the stuffy air of the main cabin where the arkers shared their evening meal. Tension crackled though the low-ceilinged room.

Lamps illuminated tight-packed groups in nooks and corners, throwing arms and chins and noses into grotesque relief. Elongated monsters leapt and danced across the walls as the shadow-casters who made them shouted and waved their arms, each determined to be heard over the other.

"So, we just move ashore? Abandon the arks?"

"We can't remain at sea forever." The ship's carpenter shook his hammer. "I can barely keep up repairs to this old tub as it is. The plan was always to return to the land."

"And if the land sinks again, Hiram? We might all drown this time."

A young woman burst into loud sobs. "The children --- what about the children?"

Jem's mam snorted. "Yes, what about the children? D'ya want them to never run and play on dry land? To never know what it feels like to live in a real home?"

"Maryam, *this* is our home."

"No. It's not." Jem's great-grandfather was shepherded to center of the room, Jem's father on one side, the captain at his shoulder. Stooped with age and slow of step, Samuel was still a commanding presence, his voice deep and resonant.

The crowds drew back to give him space, some with respect, but many in steely-eyed defiance.

Samuel stared into the familiar faces surrounding him. "I know you're afraid. I'm afraid, too. I was there. I lost my father to the storms, and his father. I saw the floods sweep away the only world I'd ever known. And I can't promise they won't come again. No-one can."

Harsh muttering swept the cabin. Samuel raised a hand for silence.

"Hiram is right, though. We never intended to live in the arks forever. But we can't abandon them. Not yet. We'll have to depend on them for a long time."

Samuel gazed round the room, catching the eye of each arker in turn.

"We all know this, but perhaps we need to hear it again: there's years of hard work ahead --- perhaps generations of it.

First, we have to return our world to a livable state. As the earth rises, we must find a site with abundant fresh water. Prepare the soil for crops. Plant trees. Then we'll need to teach the creatures in our care how to live on land. Make shelters for them. Only then can we think of building our own homes."

Heads nodded in grudging agreement.

"We must see what Ark Four's discovered. It may not even be a good place to start. But, we'll never know 'til we go and see for ourselves."

The captain raised a hand to quell the rumblings. "It's late. We're all tired. Get some rest. We'll make our plans in the morning."

As the crowd thinned, the captain drew Samuel, Hiram and Jem's father aside. "We need a few more good people."

"What about Elias and Martha? They're sound thinkers," Samuel said.

Hiram snorted. "All respect, Earth-born, but we need some doers, too."

Jem's father cocked his head; his dark eyes glimmered.

"Fitzpatrick, then, and his sister. And Aino Birgetsdottir."

Hiram scowled at Jem's father. "Are you playin' games? They're hard-nosed nay-sayers."

"All the more reason to bring them onside. Show 'em they're valued."

The captain watched the arkers leave, some in small clusters, their heads close, muttering and casting dark glances behind them.

Jem's father clapped him on the shoulder. "That went fairly well though, I thought."

The captain nodded. "Yes... too well."

"Jem. Wake up, son."

Jem's head was stuffed with cotton wool. He gave it a shake to clear it. "Ow." He struggled to sit up. His father's warm, strong hand slid behind Jem's back and propped him against something hard --- a wooden box?

Where am I?

Jem tried to look around but his eyes wouldn't open. He rubbed the crusts gluing them shut and his hand came away sticky. He blinked at his fingers, feeling stupid and light-headed. *Was that blood? His blood?*

"Saree? Mam?"

"They're alright, Jem. They're on the next raft, right beside us."

Raft?

Jem bolted upright, eyes wide, as memory rushed back in bits and flashes.

Sibilant whispers in the dark, stealthy footsteps; doors kicked in and the acrid stink of cordite as gunfire boomed and echoed through the passageways. Guns.

Jem had never heard a shot fired in anger. None of them had.

A woman cradled her dying child, a boy about his age. Jem heard a sharp, flat crack. Something hummed past his ear. The woman jerked. Her arms flailed and she crumpled face-down over the boy, their blood pooling on the deck.

Smoke and muzzle flares. Running. Hiding.

A man dragged out, kicked and stomped while his wife and daughters screamed for his blood-splattered tormentors to stop. Children crying, men and women begging for mercy as they were rounded up and set adrift on a half-dozen makeshift rafts.

Then, it was over. Only darkness, muffled sobs, the slapping of the waves against their frail craft.

"Da?"

Jem's father pulled the trembling boy onto his lap. "I've got you, Jem. It's okay. It's okay."

Except it wasn't okay. It would never be okay again.

• • •

The first fingers of dawn shredded the inky dark and shed pale, pearly light on six makeshift, wooden rafts, lashed together, wallowing in the trough of a wave. Several dozen people sprawled, unmoving, on the water-logged boards. Men, women, a few children.

Overhead a bird, a stormy petrel, scribed wide lazy circles in the brightening day. One of the men stirred. Stared sky-ward. He staggered to his feet and grabbed the tiller, his eyes fixed on the winged shape overhead. His free hand clutched a little pouch hung round his neck on a braided thong.

Through the scorching heat of the day, he bore west, following the bird. When darkness enveloped the sea, a faint murmur of life rose from the rafts. Their few morsels of food were shared, and a meager sip of water, then, nothing moved save the man,, By morning, he, too, was still. But the little flotilla kept on to the west.

The raft bumped and grated over loose shingle as rolling breakers pushed it higher up the beach.

Jem opened one eye. The sun burned overhead, but the air felt cooler. It smelled different. It smelled like -- earth.

"Da? Mam – Saree?" The others on the rafts stirred. And stared.

It wasn't much to look at. Just a barren stretch of coastline. Rocks and sand. But further inland, coarse sedge-grass tossed in the breeze and sea-birds called from their perches high in the cliff. Down the coast, a fresh-water stream carved a path to the sea. And to the south, two arks bobbed on the horizon.

Jem's father splashed towards shore, then stopped. He waded back to their raft and held out his hand. "You should be the first, Samuel."

As the little band of arkers gathered at the edge of the sand, Jem's father helped the old man ashore.

Samuel knelt in the dirt above the tide-line. He opened his shirt, untied the leather thong. Then, he sprinkled the contents of his little pouch on the ground and blended it into the sandy soil.

Home is the sailor, home from sea,

And the hunter home from the hill.

He filled his hands with the new earth and spread his arms wide. Tears streaming down his seamed face, he turned and welcomed his people home.

• • •

What Big Teeth You Have

Is this the way to Grandma's house?

"Ya gettin' on, or what?" The burly bus driver didn't mean to sound gruff and scary. But his whiskey-bass rasp was loud. His deep-set, dark eyes peered from under a bushy black unibrow. And just now, he was scowling at his next fare, a sweet-faced child clutching a large wicker basket.

Her long red scarf was pulled tight against the wind. Her voice a timid quaver. "Please, sir, is this the bus to Darkwood?"

"Sign says so, don't it?"

The girl managed a tiny smile, little more than a flicker. She heaved her heavy, napkin-covered basket up the stairs and clambered onto the first empty seat.

"Not there. Can't you read? Them are re-served fer elderlies an' th' infirm." The driver pointed at a small, faded card pinned above the front seat.

Cheeks stained bright pink, the child climbed down and made her way further back.

The driver didn't see where she ended up 'til the bus was underway. Not a seat to spare, he noted with satisfaction. Then he saw the girl squeezed next to the window, basket on her lap. With a wiry, dark-haired man leaning in close. Far too close for the bus driver's comfort. The girl's, too, from the pinched look of her.

The girl shrank back against the window and sighed. Every time she traveled to see her grandmother, some smarmy letch would single her out for his special attention. Like this one, stroking her arm. Sticking his long nose in her hair as if he were scenting his next meal. Well, she'd learned her lesson the first time. Now, she always travelled prepared.

The driver checked his rear-view again. Resolved to keep an eye on the dark-haired man. Make sure he didn't get "handsy." But when he pulled in to the last rest stop before the final leg of the journey to Darkwood, he lost sight of the pair in the crush of disembarking passengers.

· · ·

With skill born of long practice, the dark-haired man guided the girl into the woods. Away from the crowded rest area and the lights. The sounds of the chattering passengers faded behind them.

His arm tightened round her shoulders and he pulled back her scarf. "Aren't you a pretty little thing," His over-large white teeth gleamed in a wolfish smile. "And isn't this a pleasant spot. Nice and quiet. We can get to know each other better. A lot better."

The girl's eyes flew around the clearing. Towering evergreens pressed in on every side. A thick cushion of pine needles muffled the sound of their footfalls.

The dark man took the heavy basket from her arms. His smile widened and his tongue flicked out, over thin, red lips. "What's in here, girlie? Lotta nice goodies for Grandma, I'll bet."

He set the basket down and pulled back the cloth. Expecting to see fresh bread, home-made preserves, cheese and chocolate, apples and ham. Treats for a beloved grannie. Anything but what greeted his eyes.

Moonlight glinted off the keen, sharp edges of a folding shovel, a woodsman's axe, and several garden tools. He dropped the cloth and stumbled back in shock. "Holy shit, who are you?"

The girl stepped towards him, her face calm, matter-of-fact. His eyes widened in surprise. *"I may have underestimated her,"* he thought.

The last thing he saw was the well-honed axe that cleaved his skull. He would have been impressed by the short work the girl made of digging his grave. He'd always liked to linger over his prey. But she wasted no time in covering every trace of her would-be predator.

She sighed again. "Every. Single. Time."

Once she'd restored the silent clearing to its pristine beauty, the girl wiped her tools clean of blood and pine needles and returned them to her wicker basket. Covered the axe and shovel, trowel and hand-rake with the white cloth. Tied her red scarf against the chill.

The last remaining passengers were boarding when she arrived at the bus.

The driver was counting heads and checking the tally on his clipboard. "You okay, kid?"

The girl nodded and lugged her heavy basket back up the aisle to her window seat.

"Thet feller didn' try nothin', did he?" Not waiting for her reply, the driver peered out the door and continued, "Where'd he get to, anyway?"

The tiny smile flickered again. "He decided not to come the rest of the way. He'd already gone quite far enough."

The driver shrugged. "Okay fer him." He winked at the rest of the passengers in the rearview mirror. Let out the clutch and stomped on the accelerator. "Next stop, Darkwood: Grandma Holzfaller's Roadhouse."[2]

• • •

It's Just A Trick Of The Light

When we love "truly, madly, deeply", when we give our heart to another, do we truly give ourselves? When we say, "I can't live without you," is it more than some romantic, old-fashioned turn of phrase, or just another extravagant promise?

When we gaze into our lover's eyes and see ourselves reflected there, is it really a reflection we behold? Could that tiny image be, in fact, a fragment of our soul, caught and held, suspended in love's regard? Or, is it ---and, are you --- just some trick of the light?

The fire flickered fitfully. Faint, grey whisps trailed from the ancient iron grating. The strangely sweet smoke hung heavy in the air. Flames flared briefly, gilding the attic room in its rosy glow. Silken panels draping the brick walls gleamed russet and gold.

Filmy scarves in rich jewel tones spilled over the tall, hand-painted dressing screen beside the door. A bow-front chest of drawers stood under the room's only window, its embroidered dresser-scarf littered with tiny pots of rouge and lip-pomade. The satin counter-pane discarded on the floor beside the massive four-poster pooled in a shining puddle shading from palest rose highlights where the light struck just so, to blood red and midnight-burgundy in its deepest folds.

On the low, lacquered table beside the bed, a blue China bowl cradled fresh peaches next to a dish of tiny, wild strawberries lapped in heavy cream and drizzled with Phoenician honey. A wine cooler stood nearby, the empty bottle upturned in the melting ice. Twin goblets by the bed held only sweet, scarlet dregs.

The candles had been snuffed and the gaslights turned down to the barest glow. The lovers lay on cool linen sheets in the near-dark, naked limbs entwined.

"Say it," Sadie whispered, her breath warm on Jason's mouth. "Say you love me. Say you can't live without me." Her full lips nuzzled the strong column of his throat. Her long, dark curls brushed his chest.

A strand of purest silver threaded one of the luxuriant, mahogany waves. Jason teased it out and held it to his lips. "You're so beautiful."

"Am I?" Sadie's amber eyes sparkled. "It's been three months, tonight. Surely, you're tired of me by now --- old and grey as I've become?"

"One grey hair or a thousand, you shall always be my beautiful love." Jason wrapped his hands in her tousled mane as she moved lower, her mouth scorching, teasing, demanding. His flesh burned. Blood pounded in his ears as his body arched to meet her.

"Tell me." She breathed the words against his fevered skin.

He was on fire. "I love you, Sadie. Oh, God, I love you. I can't live without you." His breath rushed out in a ragged shout.

Sadie smiled and threw back her tangled curls, the familiar planes of her face smoothed, shadowed, made mysterious by the moon. She stretched, revelling as his eyes devoured her. The thickening smoke wafted over her gleaming flesh, drifted toward her lover. She sucked in its tendrils greedily. Plucking a ripe peach from the bowl on the lacquered table, she lay back against the tangle of snowy sheets; smooth, polished ebony silvered by the moon, save where the flickering light from the dying fire warmed her skin to flame-kissed, molten bronze.

Sadie bit into the peach, her strong, white teeth piercing its velvet flesh. The juice ran down her chin. She laughed and held out her arms. Offered him the succulent fruit. "Show me."

The smoke tickled Jason's throat. He felt light-headed from the fumes. He bit into the peach, then claimed Sadie's mouth.

Sadie lifted his head, her eyes locked on his. "What do you see?" As they moved together in a rhythm as old as time, Jason felt himself falling, melting into her shimmering, amber gaze.

• • •

Next morning dawned crisp and clear, warm for February. A Hansom cab clattered across the cobbles of the silent back-street and decanted two well-dressed men at the front door of a modest brownstone.

The two men checked up and down the street. Seeing no-one, they mounted the few stone stairs and knocked quietly.

An old woman, all in black save for her white cap and apron, opened the door. In response to their low-voiced inquiry, she led them up the creaking oak staircase to an attic room, unlocked the scarred wooden door and stepped aside.

The men stared. The scarlet-draped room's only occupant, a young girl clutching a too-big, figured-silk kimono around her, stared back, big-eyed, her smooth, brown face expressionless.

The younger of the two men rounded on the old woman. "Well, where are they? D'you mean to tell me they just up and left. No notice? Nothing? And this child --- whose is she? The woman's?"

The child, a beautiful girl of about eight or nine was sitting on the floor beside a black lacquered table, calmly eating a peach. She affected not to hear the men but glanced over at the old woman.

The woman's face paled. She twisted her apron in both hands, her heavy accent thickened by fear. "Your friend give money for room. Three months. Money gone, now. Friend gone. Only child here."

The older man pushed back his bowler hat and sighed. "If Jason and his lady-love have flown the coop, there's not much we can do, Carruthers. He's a grown man, who can come and go as he pleases. And his father will just have to face up to it."

Aaron Carruthers' mouth pulled down. He eyed the silent girl. "Yes, well, face up it or not, he won't be very happy, Martin."

His partner of fourteen years, Martin Ellis, was used to their clients being unhappy, for one reason or another. He didn't like it much either, but it was all part of the job. And just now, their job had been keeping tabs on young Jason because of his father's concern over this latest dalliance.

Ellis offered the woman a few coins. She shoved them in her apron pocket and raised her hand in a ritual gesture to ward off evil. Then she spat between her fingers in the direction of the child and hastily withdrew.

Ellis shrugged and started down the stairs. "Come along then."

"Wait." Carruthers rushed into the hallway and leaned over the banister to clutch Ellis' sleeve. "We can't just leave the girl here."

"Why ever not?"

"It's a brothel. It's no place for a child. Even the child of a – even *her* child."

Ellis pushed his hat back again and rubbed his forehead. Aaron was a kind man if too soft-hearted for his own good. "Well, what do you propose?"

Carruthers thought hard. "We could take her to Sisters of Mercy."

"The orphanage?" Ellis didn't believe an orphanage would offer the girl any better home than her current circumstances, but it would relieve Aaron's concern. He nodded.

"Right, then." Carruthers walked back into the room and knelt beside the girl. "You'll come with us, child. We'll take you to a safe place. Go and gather up your things, now."

The girl stared, eyes huge.

"D'you not have anything else to wear? Some other clothes to pack up?"

The child shook her head.

He patted her shoulder. She reminded him of his own dear Eliza, just going on ten. "That's alright. We'll find you something to wear. Something nice. Would you like that?"

The little girl nodded, her amber eyes fixed on Carruthers' face.

Carruthers stared. He caught the girl's chin in his hand and turned her face to the pale February sunlight streaming in the window. He leaned closer, peered into her eyes.

"What on earth are you doing?" Ellis' voice boomed in his ear.

Carruthers jumped. "I – nothing, nothing. I just – "

"Hmph." Ellis wrapped the girl in the red counter-pane and carried her down the stairs, Carruthers close behind. He thrust her into the waiting coachman's arms and pulled his partner aside. "What was that about?" he hissed.

Carruthers glanced over his shoulder towards the coach and cleared his throat. "You know how, when you look into someone's eyes, you see your reflection?"

Ellis nodded, brow furrowed.

"Well – " Carruthers pulled at his collar as if it were suddenly too tight. "When I looked into the girl's eyes, I didn't. I didn't see myself, I mean." He broke off again, eyed his partner. "You'll think me mad. I do, too. But for a moment before you spoke, I saw young Jason. In her eyes --- and I swear he saw me, too. He reached towards me as if he were calling out."

Ellis stared at Aaron. Then he looked at the waiting coach. At the young girl sitting beside the coachman, twirling a long curl in her fingers --- a dark brown strand shot through with a glint of purest silver. He took a deep breath and patted his partner's shoulder.

"You're right. It does sound mad. You must have imagined it --- a trick of the light. What other rational explanation could there possibly be?"

But as they sat the girl in the Hansom cab between them and sped towards Sisters of Mercy, neither man could bring himself to look at her. Sunk in thought, they both stared, unseeing, at the still-silent streets.

"Surely, it was just some trick of the light."

• • •

I Know What You Did

It's Halloween. Do you know where the children are?

"Alan, it's seven-thirty --- where's Robbie?"

"It's okay 'Manda. He's next door, playing. He's fine."

Amanda Sawyer took a deep breath. Smiled reassuringly into worried brown eyes staring anxiously from the mirror. "He'll be fine." The tension lines around the eyes smoothed marginally.

Amanda pursed her lips. *"Nice shade,"* she thought. *"What's it called? Oh, right. 'Autumn Glow' ."* She patted her up-swept chestnut curls one last time. "And you'll do fine, too."

She smiled again at her reflection. A bright, sparkly, 'I'm-going-to-have-such-fun-meeting-our-neighbors' smile. *"Liar."*

A hand touched her neck, feather-soft. She jumped. Saw Alan in the mirror.

He squeezed her shoulders, slid an arm around her waist and pulled her close. Solid, comforting, his breath warm against her throat.

She twisted round to face him. Gave him a peck on the cheek. "You're cute, Blondie, but don't mess my hair. I have to be perfect to meet the other wives. Perfect hair, perfect family, perfect sweet potato pie. Command performance. I have my marching orders from the company matriarch, Mrs. Welland."

Alan grimaced. "I know, I'm sorry. It's all a bit 'Stepford Wives' --- this whole 'one big happy family' Halloween picnic."

"Don't worry. If they drug the pumpkin-spice lattes, we're outa there, pie and all." Amanda laughed. Startled by the happy sound, she froze. Then shivered at a sudden thought. "Alan, they don't have a pool?"

Alan's shoulders slumped. "No, 'Manda, there's no pool. I promise."

"Because if there's a pool, we can't go. Robbie can't be there. Not ever. Not after Sara..." Rising panic tightened her voice.

"I know, Amanda, I know! Robbie can't be near water. God, I know - " Alan's voice cracked. He mastered his ragged breathing, managed a strained smile. "There's no pool. Now please, can we just go?"

Slow tears leaked from under Amanda's lashes. Alan wrapped his arms around her. "It'll be alright. I promise."

• • •

The children were seated in a ragged circle in the center of the tree-house. Robbie had never been in a tree-house before. It was pretty cool, high in the crotch of a huge, old oak tree. With a balcony and rope ladder. Floor cushions. Blankets. Solar-powered lanterns. Just the right size for kids.

His dad had promised to build one, but then they'd moved here.

Robbie's eyes flicked to the pinched, freckled face of the girl across from him.

Nona Fielding's stick-straight red hair refused to be confined in the single braid hanging down her back. It stuck out around her face in a ragged, static-fueled halo. Her dark blue jumper was streaked with jam from one of the stolen pastries. The rest were being devoured by her partners in crime.

"They taste better when you steal 'em," she'd said.

Robbie took a tentative bite of his. It was still warm. Raspberry. Not his favorite, but not bad. Though he didn't see the point of taking something when it would've been given to him anyway.

The twins, Sam and Jorge, were making a mess of their matching white shirts and hand-knit sweater vests. They dressed just like their dad, with the same round, steel-rimmed glasses and bow ties. Ten-year-old baby business robots.

What had his dad called their father? *"Oh, yeah. A chicken-neck bean-counter."* Robbie giggled at the thought of a scrawny chicken head sticking out of Mr. Canavan's suit.

"What're *you* laughing at?"

Nona's sharp, spite-laden question snapped Robbie's eyes back to her face. *"Uh-oh, better be careful."* He blinked, smiled tentatively. "I was wondering -- " He waved his pastry towards the Ouija board in the center of their circle. "How does that work? Is it fun?"

Nona grabbed the planchette protectively. "You put your fingers on it and ask questions. It's not for babies."

"I'm not a baby. I'm almost nine."

"Ha! I'm eleven. Even Helen's older'n you."

Robbie glanced at Helen Trask, Nona's silent shadow. Blond, soft Helen never spoke unless Nona told her to. She stared back at Robbie, blank-faced, as if waiting for Nona to tell her what to say.

Nona glanced around the circle. "First, we play 'Truth or Dare'." The other three leaned in, eyes avid. They knew what was coming.

"And you get to go first."

Robbie felt the other children holding their breath. He finished his pastry and brushed the crumbs off his bright, orange tee. "Okay."

A sigh ran through the little group. Nona smiled. Her pink tongue flicked across her moist lower lip.

"Okay. What are you most scared of?"

Robbie stared at the Ouija board. Once she knew his biggest fear, he'd be at Nona's mercy. He felt the jaws of the trap yawning wide. *But maybe...*"

"Katy-did."

Nona snorted. "You're afraid of a little, green grasshopper?" The twins snickered.

"No, not a grasshopper. Katy-did." Robbie pointed at the planchette clutched in Nona's hand. "I can show you."

He felt Nona's confidence waver. She hadn't expected his response and wasn't quite sure what to do. Robbie waited.

Nona plunked the three-cornered, wooden tripod down on the board. "Fine. Show me."

The jaws of the trap snapped shut. A gust of wind ripped through the tree-house, rattling dying leaves against the walls, flapping the hand-lettered "Keep Out" and "No Babies Allowed" posters.

The twins jumped. Helen shivered and rubbed her sweater-clad arms.

Robbie placed his fingers on the wooden planchette. He looked at Nona.

Nona's chin jutted as she placed her fingers on the tripod next to Robbie's. For a moment, nothing happened. "You have to ask a question." Nona's scorn prickled Robbie's skin.

"Are you here?" he asked. Nothing. "Katy-did, are you here?"

The red ball of the sun dropped behind dark clouds billowing on the horizon. Another gust moaned through the tree-house. The planchette stirred. Slowly at first, then gaining speed, it glided smoothly across the board, pointing out letters.

i.a.m.k.a.t.y.d.i.d.i.a.m.h.e.r.e.

Nona ripped the tripod from Robbie's hands. "You did that!"

Robbie sat back. "Ask one of them." He nodded towards the other three. "Ask 'em all. Don't matter. Katy-did's here."

Helen whimpered. "It's dark. I'm supposed to go home when it's dark."

"Shut up, baby. You can go home when I say." Nona snapped the switch on one of the old, solar-powered lanterns. "That's why we have these."

The twins quickly followed suit with the other three lights. In the yellow-green glare, the children's faces were sallow, drawn.

"Ask again," Robbie challenged. "Dare you." The wind sighed through the old tree, rattling the leaves.

Nona glowered, but placed the wooden tripod on the board. "Sam, you and Jorge do it."

The twins reluctantly placed their fingertips on the planchette.

i.a.m.k.a.t.y.d.i.d.i.k.n.o.w.w.h.a.t.y.o.u.d.i.d.s. a.m.

Sam eyes flashed. He yanked his hands back and slugged his brother's arm.

"Ow! That hurt, you jerk."

"You promised you'd never tell anyone I took it. You swore."

"I never said a word." Jorge rubbed his shoulder. The twins scowled at each other and drew apart. The old oak tree's branches rubbed and groaned.

Nona pounced on the tripod. "Took what? What did Sam take?" She grabbed Helen's wrist. "Help me."

A sudden rush of wind-driven leaves whispered and chattered across the tree-house floor. Helen's staring eyes were all pupil, huge and black. She wrenched her hand free. "No! I won't"

The planchette spun from Nona's grasp and flew across the board.

i.a.m.k.a.t.y.d.i.d.i.k.n.o.w.w.h.a.t.y.o.u.d.i.d.h.e.l.e.n.

"No, Nona. I didn't mean it. They made me. Please, Nona, don't be mad." Helen's teary-eyed pleas enraged Nona.

"You told on me?" Nona launched herself at the frightened girl, shrieking and slapping. "They took away my computer --- for a whole week!"

Helen fell backwards. Her head hit the floor with a sharp crack. She lay unresponsive, flopping like a rag-doll with each blow.

"Nona, stop! Stop it." Shouting to Robbie to run for help, Sam and Jorge pulled Nona away from Helen. Tried to hold her as she kicked and thrashed.

In the scuffle, one of the lanterns fell against the door curtain, its bulb white-hot. The nylon fabric darkened at its touch. As Robbie clambered down the ladder, the curtain began to smoke and smolder.

Robbie reached the ground and looked up at the tree-house, then at the rope in his hands. He gave a sharp yank. The old ladder shredded and fell away.

Flames sprang up as the curtain and then the pillows burst into flames. Terrified shrieks floated down to Robbie. "Help!" "Where's the ladder?" "Robbie, help us!" "Help!" "Mommy!" "Dad! Daddy --- help!"

The boy cocked his head. Over the screaming, over the silky, hungry, crackling of the fire, he could hear the planchette hissing across the board.

i.a.m.k.a.t.y.d.i.d.i.k.n.o.w.w.h.a.t.y.o.u.d.i.d.r.
o.b.b.i.e.

With a whooshing roar that drowned out the children's cries, the huge tree top blazed up.

The grownups would be there soon. They were already shouting, running across the lawn towards the tree-house. Somebody'd called the fire department. Their sirens wailed in the distance.

Robbie smiled. He liked fire engines.

• • •

Amanda shivered. She was cold. So very, very cold. The heat from the huge, brightly burning Halloween bonfire couldn't warm her.

Across the lawn, the flames were doused. The oak tree released it's victims. The wailing of the sirens died as ambulances crews called to the scene quickly realized the children were beyond all mortal help.

Parents wept in each other's arms or huddled in dazed silence, trying to absorb the awful truth.

Amanda's eyes searched the crowds for Alan. He'd be in the thick of it, trying to help. Trying to offer comfort where there was no real comfort to be found.

She looked down at her little son. He was standing beside her, quietly impaling another marshmallow on his forked stick. His face a study in concentration as he calmly rotated the sweet over a glowing ember at the edge of the blaze, carefully toasting it to an even, golden brown. Then he removed it from the stick and placed it at the end of the row. Six perfectly golden marshmallows. He reached in the bag.

Amanda knelt beside Robbie. "Aren't you going to eat them?"

"No. I just like to toast them."

"Maybe you could leave some for somebody else?"

"I don't think they want any." Robbie flicked a glance at the flashing lights and milling crowd across the park. "They're pretty busy."

Amanda shivered again. She took Robbie by the shoulders. Turned him to face her. "So *beautiful. My angelic, boy-child --- blond and slim and beautiful, so like your daddy,"* Amanda thought, her heart breaking.

Robbie stared at her, hazel eyes wide, guileless.

"What happened, Robbie?"

"It was Katy-did."

Amanda's heart jolted. *"Dear God, not again."* A band of iron clamped her chest. Squeezed. Black spots floated before her eyes. She shook her head, willing her vision to clear. "Katy-did."

"Yes." Robbie threaded another marshmallow onto his stick.

"Like when Sara – " Amanda's throat closed.

"Yes." Robbie fiddled with the marshmallow. "Katy-did told Sara to see if she could swim 'til Daddy came. She couldn't."

Amanda forced the words past clenched teeth. "But I was there, Robbie. I was at home. Why didn't you call me?"

Her fingers were crushing the boy's orange tee-shirt, squeezing his arms. She knew, vaguely, on some level, she must be hurting him, but he never moved. She wanted to scream and shake him. "Why didn't you call me?"

Robbie looked at her blankly. "Because I wanted to see, too."

Her breath gusted out in a ragged whisper. "And the tree-house? Your friends?"

Robbie's eye reflected silver in the flickering light. "We were finished playing. So I climbed down. Katy-did said they didn't need the ladder."

Amanda nodded. "I see." She gently removed the toasting stick from his hands.

The little boy looked confused. "I'm not finished, yet."

"It's okay, Robbie. Come with me. Just for a minute." She hugged Robbie to her, wrapping his legs about her waist, clasping his little-boy arms round her neck. She folded her arms tightly around him. The little boy squirmed. "It's okay, Robbie. This will only take a minute."

In one smooth motion, Amanda stood and walked straight into the heart of the bonfire with her son.

As the flames enveloped them, Robbie's screams pierced the night. He twisted frantically in her arms. Arching his back, trying to break free. "No, Mommy, no! It hurts! Mommy, stop! Stop! Daddy --- Daddy!"

Their skin began to bubble and char. Robbie smashed his head against her. Amanda felt her nose break. Hot blood gushing down her face. Her hair blazed up. Robbie kicked and bit, tearing, clawing. Thrashing wildly. Screaming for Alan.

Amanda crushed her son to her chest. *"Tighter. Tighter. Don't let go!"* She felt their flesh melting together. Their bones were white-hot, incandescent.

Over the roaring in her ears, she heard voices. Shocked. Horrified.

"My God, stop her." "Grab her!" "Get them out of there." "She's burning him alive!" "How can she do that to her own child?" "Jesus, God, somebody do something."

She felt her son's life flutter, flicker out.

She turned. Saw Alan. Struggling between two fire fighters, screaming her name. Trying to come to her. She smiled. "*I love you. I will always love you.*"

The last thing she saw was Alan sinking to his knees, sobbing, tears mingled with the soot streaking his face, still reaching for her as her bones cracked and crumbled to ash.

• • •

Katy-did looked down at the spirit of the beautiful boy-child standing calmly in the dark. He seemed fascinated by the lights, the police-radios, the crush of people round the dying pyre, the crumpled forms at its heart.

i.a.m.k.a.t.y.d.i.d.

"I know."

y.o.u.r.m.o.t.h.e.r.g.a.v.e.y.o.u.t.o.t.h.e.f.i.r.e.

"She gave me to you."

133

Katy-did thought about that for a moment. s.h.e.d.i.d.n.t.m.e.a.n.t.o.

The spirit-boy shrugged. "But, giving me to the fire gave me to you."

Katy-did flexed its wings. a.r.e.y.o.u.r.e.a.d.y.

"For what?" The spirit raised silver eyes to the Kay-did's face.

i.t.s.h.a.l.l.o.w.e.e.n.s.h.a.l.l.w.e.f.i.n.d.s.o.m.e. m.o.r.e.c.h.i.l.d.r.e.n.t.o.p.l.a.y.w.i.t.h.

The spirit smiled. "I'd like that."

Katy-did raised its wings. The silver-eyed spirit climbed on Katy-did's back. They shimmered and faded. Flew across the lawn in a rush of wind.

The crowds shivered as the icy gust swept over them, sending sparks swirling high into the night sky from the fading embers of the Halloween bonfire.

• • •

The Butterfly Man

You don't have to be a new broom to clean up

6:03 A.M.

The disused basement room was cool and dry. Dim light filtered though the narrow slats of the ventilation louvers high on the north wall, casting barred shadows across the room. The collector had chosen it for the north light --- artists' light. Pure and unaltered by the heat of the day or changing seasons.

He gazed at his children, suspended in a neat row from an overhead beam. That's how he thought of them --- his children. Not by blood or birth, but by careful curation. — Sadly, only a few would become the beautiful butterflies he knew they could be. And he abhorred to waste a single one. It drove him to refine his selection process. He'd watch for months before deciding. Observe and record. Only then were they collected. Cocooned. Made ready for their metamorphosis. — The collector's keen eye spotted a few shreds of fabric near the door-

135

jamb. He must have tracked them in without noticing. He cursed his carelessness and grabbed an old push-broom from the corner. Scrubbed his boot-soles against it. Then swept up the fragments and tucked them in his pocket for later disposal.

10:17 A.M.

Principal Rodman fiddled with his shiny, new nameplate. Ran a nervous hand over his immaculate shirt-front. His dark hair was brushed. Shoes shined. His tie was straight. He'd checked several times. First loosening the knot for a casual effect. Then tightening it, because casual might be seen as untidy.

He knew why the Chair of the School Board had insisted on meeting. Rodman was the 'new broom'. Expected to sweep through the well-waxed hallways and 'clean house'. And the Board Chair was coming to let Rodman know what needed to be swept away.

Manila files sat stacked on his desk. Couriered to the newly-appointed principal in advance of the meeting. He lifted the cover of the top-most folder. Surveyed the list of proposed budget 'modifications'. The longer list of 'staff redundancies'.

Rodman had already been approached by a few senior teachers about early retirement. But cutting a third of his teachers, curtailing all extra-curricular activities and reducing support to a bare minimum was a lot to chew on.

Just now though, Rodman was preoccupied with fourteen missing students. Vanished from neighboring schools over the past year. Three in the last week. They concerned Rodman more than a balanced budget. Though as none of his students were missing --- yet --- Rodman doubted they'd make the agenda.

A brisk knock interrupted his ruminations. The receptionist poked her head round the edge of the door.

"Mr. Pettigrew from the School Board is here."

Short and pudgy 'Mr. Pettigrew from the School Board', resplendent in a navy-blue three-piece barged past her. "Thank you, Miss Jones."

Miss Jones rolled her eyes and withdrew.

Rodman rose. Offered his hand. "Mr. Pettigrew – "

Pettigrew ignored him. Plopped into a chair across from Rodman and perched an old-fashioned pince-nez on the bridge of his nose. "Let's get down to it."

An hour later, he and Rodman were still dead-locked over the first item on Pettigrew's agenda. Firing the school's venerable custodian.

"But Mr. Gutierrez has been with us since ---"

Pettigrew frowned. "Since Moses was in short pants. Yes. He's a fixture. And I'm sure he's loved by all. But even a well-loved fixture eventually outlives its usefulness."

"Actually, there have been a few complaints. Nothing serious. A leaky faucet in the staff bathroom. Burnt out lights in the girls' change room."

Pettigrew leaned back and steepled his fingers. "What about his refusal to sweep out the science lab. And forgetting to lock the court-yard door?'

So, the board knew about that... "Well, yes. And the broom thing – "

"The 'broom thing'?" Pettigrew's eyebrows almost met his receding hair-line.

Rodman shifted in his seat. Decades of staff meetings had perfected Rodman's poker-face. But he couldn't escape feeling as if he were a naughty school-boy, summoned to the principal's office.

"It was nothing, really. A misunderstanding. The Automotive Club used one of Mr. G.'s brooms. He was upset it was returned covered in grease and oil."

Pettigrew's eyes bulged. "Principal Rodman, a dirty broom is the least of your problems. Your science department has lodged several complaints with the board." Pettigrew shook his head. "Clearly, the custodian must go."

So, Carmichael sicced the board on him. "If we could just just sit down with Mr. Gutierrez..."

The board chair rose. Made a show of polishing his pince-nez. "You have twenty-four hours. Then, I expect him gone. Good day."

Rodman sighed. So much for discussing the missing students.

3:18 P. M.

The sun tracked round towards the west, across the afternoon sky. Below, in the basement room, barred light from the ventilators fell across the last cocoon in the row. She arched her back. Twisted her body 'til she felt the comforting warmth on her face.

Far-away voices filtered through the vent. Care-free, school's-out-for-the-day laughter. Shoes crunching on gravel walkways.

A low moan escaped the bindings securing her mouth. The pounding in her head made it hard to think. She'd no idea how long she'd been hanging there. Or where 'there' was. But she knew she wasn't alone. The sound of labored breathing on either side filled each waking moment.

At first, she'd heard screams, wild thrashing, crying. Then he'd come and dragged the screamer away. After that, the rest were quiet.

Or dying. Would she be dead soon? Or would she feel the sun again tomorrow?

She let herself drift 'til the warmth faded and the voices died away.

8:30 P.M.

Walter Gutierrez man-handled the unwieldy, industrial floor-washer down the empty hallway. Gave it an extra-hard shove to maneuver round a corner. "Self-propelled, my ass, you piece a' junk."

He poked his head into the Mr. Carmichael's science lab. Sure enough, chairs and stools stood ready at each workstation. He backed out, muttering under his breath. "You don't stack the damn chairs, I don't clean yer damn floors."

His last name, Gutierrez, meant 'he who rules' and Walter reigned supreme in all matters janitorial. First and foremost, one simple rule --- 'everything off the floors'. No pick-up, no clean-up.

Walter's second rule, 'don't touch my stuff,' covered everything from cleaning supplies to hand-tools --- and, of course, his brooms. The brooms were his first line of defense against the chaos.

He stowed the heavy washer in the equipment locker and headed out on his evening rounds. Basements first and all the connecting tunnels. Courtyard and outbuildings last.

9:17 P.M.

The door to the secluded basement room swung open with a faint creak. The collector stepped inside. Light from the hallway washed over the fourteen cocoons in their neat row.

One of them stirred. Sensing the light, she struggled against the bindings securing her to the rafter.

"Shh, shh. Your time will come very soon, now. Be still, child."

The bundled form let out a high-pitched moan which rose to a muffled shriek. The cocoon beside it began to jerk and wail as well. Then a third.

"Go ahead, then, if you must. Scream. Cry. Call for help. No-one will hear you."

The basement door crashed back on its hinges. "I heard them."

The collector was swept off his feet by an old push broom. Seconds later the handle broke his jaw in two places and knocked him senseless.

4:21 A.M.

Three men stood in the middle of the schoolyard, shoulders hunched against the cold pre-dawn air. They watched the last ambulance roll away, sirens blaring. Rushing to reunite the few lucky survivors with their families.

The dead children had been removed. And the police had carted off the 'collector' in handcuffs, protesting his innocence through clenched teeth and a taped-up jaw.

"You think he'll get off?"

Rodman shook his head. "They found bits of the cocoon material in his pocket and all over the floor of his science lab. Plus, they'll have Mr. G.'s testimony."

Pettigrew's shiver had little to do with the early-morning chill. "I never would have believed it. Carmichael was such a likeable fellow."

"That's what they said about Ted Bundy."

Pettigrew frowned. Squared his shoulders and turned to the caretaker. "You're a hero, Mr. Gutierrez. I don't see how we can ever let you go, now. But, I'm curious. What made you suspect Carmichael?"

Gutierrez shrugged. "I didn't. But he's here at very strange hours for a teacher. And he makes trouble for me. So, I follow him to see what he's doing. Maybe make some trouble for him."

Rodman offered the broken pieces of the old broom to their newly-permanent custodian.

"Well, Mr. G., you solved the crime of the decade and saved the lives of three of the kidnapped children. What's next?"

Walter grunted. He hefted the broken handle. "I'm gonna fix this. Don't have to be a new broom to sweep good."

• • •

Sleeping Beauty

"Home, where my thought's escaping, Home, where my music's playing, Home, where my love lies waiting Silently for me" --- Paul Simon

The old Simon and Garfunkel piece floated to the surface of her mind. She listened for a moment, the guitars jangled in the background. The words bobbed past in the stream of her consciousness, mauve and palest, Easter-egg pink --- a few with yellow and green stripes.

Was I having an episode? My doctor told me synesthesia isn't real, but every time I hear certain songs, I see coloured words. And, I can taste the colours--- spicy hot, or smooth and cool, dancing on my tongue –

She felt *him*.

"Is that you?" *He's here --- I know it.* "Are you here, my Adam?"

She felt him, closer now, close enough almost to touch. "Are you here, love?"

She wasn't altogether sure where "here" was -- sometimes it was ink-black. An icy slab beneath her and downward-dragging darkness seeping into her core, pulling her to never-ending night. "*Am I dead?*" she wondered.

No, not dead. Waiting. Waiting for the light to come again. Waiting -- for him?

And then, she heard it. Birdsong. She felt cool, lush grass under her feet. Dappled light streamed through the leafy canopy to warm her skin. The scent of lavender, sharp-tasting yet sweet, washed over her.

And wherever this truly was, this "here", she knew her Adam would find her.

• • •

"Can she hear me?" The young intern leaned closer. Flicked his tiny, bright light across the young woman's partially open eyes.

"Hmm. Unresponsive. Make a note, please, nurse."

The young woman lay unmoving. The only signs of life were the regular sounds of her breathing and the beeping and chirping of the monitors attached to her head and body. And, in spite of her unnatural, ashy paleness, there was something attractive, almost seductive about the dark-haired form.

I dutifully recorded his assessment on the chart. Added it to the long list of other such observations.

He adjusted one of the monitors, checked its readings, reached for her wrist to take her pulse.

"Don't touch her." I rapped out the words, sharp, unthinking.

He yanked his hand back and stared at me.

Back up, girl. Don't push too hard. It'll only make him stubborn. "Sorry, doctor. It's just, she doesn't respond well to physical stimuli. It agitates her. It's in her charts, doctor."

I help out my clipboard. The patient file was thick with notes --- confused diagnoses, possible prognoses.

The young doctor thumbed through the pages, pausing here and there to mutter a few words. I knew what the charts contained --- I'd written most of the notes as senior Case Nurse since the comatose young woman we'd dubbed "Sleeping Beauty" had been admitted over a year ago.

They were still trying to figure out what was wrong and how to fix it. So far, her doctors agreed on very little --- except the seizures. "No rise in electrical activity recorded. NES --- nonepileptic seizures? Physical contact for routine procedures appears to cause extreme stress. Possible dissociative disorder?"

The seizures only happened when the female nursing staff carried out their daily routine: vital signs, bed bath, changing the linens. Almost as if the patient couldn't bear the touch of another woman.

He handed back the chart. "Thank you, nurse." He fussed with one of the dials until the reading was adjusted to his satisfaction.

I realized he was saving face. Showing me who was in charge. So, I waited, face carefully neutral.

But as we strode down the long corridor to check on the rest of our patients, I saw his stealthy backwards glance at Sleeping Beauty's door. I pretended not to notice, but I should have kept an eye on him after rounds. And I should never have let him go back alone.

• • •

The young doctor checked up and down the hall for the nurse. *No-one in sight*. He slipped into the room and crossed to the still form on the bed.

Her hand was warm. Her fingers stirred in his and suddenly, he was staring into sparkling, black-diamond eyes. He felt light-headed as if he were falling into their gaze.

"You came, my Adam. You came."

A soft voice whispered in his ear. Warm lips caressed his neck, nuzzling, nibbling. Music played in the background, guitars, two men singing. He didn't recognize the song, but the tune was pleasant, folksy.

"Where – where are we?"

They reclined together on a gilded platform spread with satin sheets. Embroidered scarlet dragons twined and curled across their silken mattress. Glowing, phoenix-blazoned banners fluttered in a canopy high above them.

He looked into her eyes and nothing else mattered save her touch. He ran his hand over the smooth curve of her hip, revelling in her soft, naked flesh. He bent and captured her mouth with his.

The gold and scarlet shimmered, faded into leafy, dappled green. They lay on a petal-strewn bower. Light breezes cooled his skin.

His cupped her breasts; lowered his head to tongue and tease her nipples. Licked and nibbled his way lower.

She moaned and arched against him. Clutched his hair, she guided him to her secret places. Tongue laved, fingers delved, plundering her velvet core. Her thighs opened wide, welcoming, then flexed and shivered. Her flesh burned under his touch.

Her hand grasped him, cupping, sliding, stroking. Silken friction. He felt her scorching lips engulf him. Sucking, eager. He cried out as she milked him.

Lips and tongue, molten-hot mouth urged him to rise again. She impaled herself on his still-willing shaft.

Fire raced along his veins as she flung back her cloud of night-dark hair and rode him, hard. Their passion flamed across the midnight sky.

Buried inside her, thrusting, pounding, he clutched her buttocks and strained after her. Wave after glorious, lavender wave of pleasure crashed over him, flooding his senses with the smell and the taste and the touch of her.

The night became her clamping, pulsing sheath, wet and burning, drawing him in, pulling him ever deeper.

He surged against her, every sinew taut, gasping, falling into her – falling into velvet dark –

• • •

I knew something was wrong when I couldn't find him after rounds. I padded down the empty hallway to her room and flung open the door. Too late –

I looked at the young man lying dead on the floor --- a dried, shrunken husk. His empty, lifeless eyes still turned towards the young woman in the bed. His outstretched hand still reaching to clasp her slender fingers in his.

A full moon cast strange, indigo shadows across the room, bathing her translucent flesh in its silvery light.

Her alabaster-pale skin glowed with the blush of life. The single sheet draped her body. Clung to breast and thigh, limning every curve and mound and secret hollow with the silken touch of a lover's hand. Her limbs exuded a heavy, sated languor. Her lips dewy-soft, rose-stained as if she'd just dined on fresh strawberries.

I twitched the extra coverlet from the foot of her bed and draped it over the young man's desiccated remains. Then, I picked up his feet and dragged his feather-light corpse into the hallway. No sense leaving him in her room for the next damn fool to traipse in --- looking for him and finding her instead.

Me, I don't care what the shrinks call it. Folie à deux; shared psychosis --- he's the third intern this year we've lost to 'Sleeping Beauty', or 'Patient X', or whatever the hell her name is.

Up to me, I'd put her in the old locked ward in the basement and throw away the key. Freakin' vampire.

• • •

Fan Club

The only constant in life is change, but some changes take a bit of getting used to

The old-fashioned, heavy, metal ceiling fan barely stirred the air over the bed. Michelle lay on top of the covers in the stifling New Orleans summer evening, staring up at the blades.

Swoosh, swoosh, swoosh, tink

She counted the revolutions. The swoop of the blades was regular, almost hypnotic. Well, except for the slight wobble in one of the blades and the tiny, metallic ping it made as its inner-end tagged the housing each time around.

Michelle's suitcase lay open on the bench, her clothes spilling onto the floor. She'd barely started unpacking when the fighting kicked up -- again.

This trip was supposed to bring them together to enjoy something they loved. New Orleans, great music, amazing food.

Having a travel writer for a mom was usually pretty great. And Aunt Jenna's foody-blog was the go-to for tourists looking for the very best in local cuisine of the places she'd visited. It had made for some awesome trips; the three of them experiencing the sights and sounds and tastes of the world.

Swoosh, swoosh, swoosh, tink

Michelle concentrated on the fan blades, trying to block out the angry voices in the adjoining room.

"Look, Lexie. I get it. It's a choice and I respect that, but – "

"But?" Her mom's normally, sweet-as-Georgia-peaches drawl was high, tight, clipped. "But what, Jenna? But y'all don't approve?"

"I didn't say that." Aunt Jenna's voice was thick, angry.

Michelle tried to focus on the wonky fan blade.

Swoosh, swoosh, swoosh, tink

"You don't have to. You used to be her biggest fan, cheerin' her on, tellin' her she could do anythin' she set her mind to. But now, you can barely look at Shell. You haven't seen her for almost a year, and you hardly spoke to her durin' the flight. Four hours and what? Two, maybe three words? 'Hey, kid how are y'all?' Oh, sorry, that's five."

"Lexie --- it's –

"What, Jenn? What? Spit it out!"

Swoosh, swoosh, swoosh, tink

"Lexie, don't. This is hard enough already?"

"Hard? Hard for me? For Shell? Or hard for you?"

Swoosh, swoosh, swoosh, tink

"It's a big change. I can't even begin to understand how difficult this has been for everyone. I just need some time to process it all."

"Process what? Y'already knew. We've been talkin' about it all year. Textin' about how well it's goin' and how happy Shell is. Sendin' photos. Process what, Jenn?"

Swoosh, swoosh, swoosh, tink

"Seeing the change is --- it's different. I knew but --- "

" 'The' change? It's *her* change, Jenna. Her change. Her transition. And you can barely look at her. Can't even say her name, can you?"

Swoosh,

"What? Of course, I – "

Swoosh

"Say it, Jenn. Say her name.

Swoosh

"Jenna, say 'Michelle'."

Swoosh

"Micah. Lexie, his name is Micah. Not 'her', not Michelle... Him. Micah."

Tink

Michelle's world stopped. It was white --- cold in spite of the sweltering heat. Empty except for the slow, jolting, thud of her heart. Her breath rasped; scorched her throat. The angry voices in the next room stabbed her ears, sharp and painful.

"Jenna – "

"Lexie, when that boy hit on Micah at the airport, hit on your son, my nephew, it was disgusting."

"He didn't see Micah, Jenn. He saw Michelle. He saw her for what she is --- a beautiful young woman. He hit on Michelle."

Swoosh, swoosh, swoosh

Michelle stared at the fan, trying to shut out the voices. Willing herself to concentrate. "*Think about the fan. Just the fan.*" The voices dropped to an indistinct murmur.

Swoosh, swoosh, swoosh, tink

Maybe she could fix it. Stop the wobble. Maybe a heavy weight would straighten the back end of the blade enough.

"Hmm. My suitcase?" she muttered. "Nope. Didn't pack enough. Auntie Jenn's suitcase would be perfect. She always packed enough for three people, but, well, I'm can't just waltz in and ask to borrow it right now. Only thing heavy enough is me."

Swoosh, swoosh, swoosh, tink

Michelle cast about for a cord, something strong enough to loop over the housing end of the blade and hold her weight. "Curtain ties. Perfect."

Swoosh, swoosh, swoosh, tink

Michelle climbed up on her bed. *"Nope, not tall enough."* She dragged the covers off, dumped her suitcase on the floor and hoisted the luggage bench into the middle of the bed, directly under the fan.

Swoosh, swoosh, swoosh, tink

She knotted the curtain ties together and formed a large noose at one end. "Okay, looks good."

Swoosh, swoosh, swoosh, tink

Michelle climbed up and looped the noose over the wonky blade. Then she slid her torso through it. The fan groaned and shuddered to a stop, then with a jerk, it started circling again.

Michelle cried out as she slipped through the loop. The braided rope snagged one arm and caught under her chin. She clawed at it, with her free hand, but couldn't get any purchase. Her struggles only pulled the noose tighter. She couldn't make a sound; could barely breathe.

Swoosh

She was slowly but surely choking. *What a stupid way to go. Death by ceiling fan.*

Swoosh

Everything was getting dark.

Swoosh

Michelle gave a last, feeble kick. Her foot caught the bench, sending it crashing to the floor.

Swoosh

• • •

"Shell, can you hear me? Michelle?" Her mother's face swam into view.

Michelle was lying on the floor, cradled in her Auntie Jenna's arms. Her mother stood over her, holding the curtain-tie noose.

"What on earth were you thinking?" she asked. Her face was parchment white, lips pinched.

"I was trying to fix the fan," Michelle croaked.

"By hanging yourself from it?"

"Well, I would have borrowed Auntie Jenn's suitcase, but you guys were – "

Her aunt's voice cut her off, "Being stupid. I was, I mean. And I'm sorry for everything you probably heard, Michelle."

Michelle's mom helped her over to the bed while her aunt retrieved the bench. She replaced Michelle's suitcase and piled her clothes on top.

"Y'all could hang these up, you know. Unless you're goin' for that slept-in-my-clothes look." She paused, glanced at Michelle. "Well, maybe tomorrow's soon enough. Throat sore?"

Michelle nodded. Her mother's hand smoothing the short, brown curls back from Michelle's forehead felt cool, soothing.

"Auntie Jenna and I'll fetch you some ice cream. For your throat. Mint chip?"

Michelle swallowed tentatively. "*Ouch.*" Ice cream would feel really good. "Yes, please."

"But, no fan fixing while we're gone. Promise?"

"I promise."

Michelle lay back on her pillows. As her mom and Auntie Jenn headed down the hall towards the hotel restaurant, their conversation floated back to her.

"My God, Lexie, she's as crazy as you were."

"*She*." Just that one word in her auntie's voice made Michelle feel all warm inside.

"Hey, I'm not the one who drove Dad's lawn tractor through the side of the barn when she was six."

"I was seven. And I couldn't reach the brakes."

"Ha. No excuse."

"Really? Well, whose bright idea was it to soap up Mom's convertible and drive it through the pond to rinse it off, 'stead of usin' buckets and a hose?"

"Billy Poe thought it was a good idea."

"Billy Poe was an idiot. And not much help when the car filled with water."

As their voices faded, Michelle looked up at the fan.

Swoosh, swoosh, swoosh, tink

It's wobble was a little worse, but otherwise, it seemed unscathed. A jazz riff wafted up from the street below.

"You know, fan," she smiled. "I think this is going to be a great trip after all."

Swoosh, swoosh, swoosh, tink

• • •

The Cat Who Thought He Could Fly

Ay caramba, Martha, get that cat a parachute

"Martha --- the cat's in my sweater drawer again." The huge marmalade cat named "Cat" opened one eye. He regarded me for a moment, as only a cat could who knew he was master of all he surveyed.

He'd wandered in one rainy afternoon almost twelve years ago. A soggy, self-assured little fur-ball. Our son, Jamie, took a shine to him.

At nine, Jamie had a big heart. He'd named the fluffy, mottled-orange kitty Mrs. Cat. When time revealed a pair of balls on Mrs. Cat's fluffy butt, Jamie changed kitty's name to "Cat --- Just Plain Cat."

J.P. Cat, or Cat for short, turned out to be a character. Given to un-cat-like behavior. Martha once suggested he could be the reincarnation of her dear, departed Uncle Thaddeus.

Her uncle had been a mite peculiar, too. Not enough to need care, but one you'd want to keep an eye on. One hot July morning, he pawned the family silver to fund an expedition to the South Pole. Made it as far Bing's Casino on his snowshoes. He won enough to get the silver outta hawk. So, no foul, I say.

But I digress. Cat liked to sleep in my sweater drawer. But he was particular. He'd paw through the sweaters 'til he found my favorite ---a new, navy blue cashmere. Then he'd curl up on it and doze off.

If I was wearing the sweater, he'd follow me around the house demanding I sit down so he could curl up on me.

As well, Cat loved the water. He'd sit on the edge of a sink and watch a tap drip for hours. He took to perching at the edge of my koi pond, patting the ripples with his paw. We thought he was fishing 'til one day we saw him slide into the water and paddle for the other shore. Then he'd turned around and paddled back.

After a good shake, he went to dry out in my sweater drawer. Which explained why every sweater I'd taken out in the past two weeks had been damp.

But the craziest thing Cat's ever done, to date, anyway, was try to fly.

It all started with the bird's nest Jamie had found on a nature hike with his Junior Rangers troop. It'd been blown down in the last big storm. Big enough for an eagle. Cat figgered it was a perfect Cat-bed.

The next morning though, Cat was nowhere to be found. Then I heard Martha scream. She'd spotted Cat strolling round on the roof.

"Get the ladder. He'll fall."

"Nope. He'll come down when he's hungry."

Jamie pleaded. Martha moped. I was adamant. Cat spent the day on the roof, bird watching. That night, he reappeared in time for supper, and a long nap in his Cat-nest-bed. Next morning, he was back up on the roof.

He lay there, stretched on his belly. Eyes fixed on the nestlings in our apple tree. I spent hours at the window. Watching Cat watch the parents teach their baby birds how to fly. I wondered if it was a hunting technique. If so, he was playing the long game.

That night we wakened to scratching noises. Something being dragged across the floor. We tiptoed down the hallway, thinking we'd surprise the noisiest burglars in creation. *Not so.*

Cat was moving his nest. He dragged it up the stairs and out the low, second-floor dormer window. Then onto the roof overhang.

"Do something. He'll fall."

Jamie pleaded. Martha moped. I caved. Next morning, I built a sturdy window-ledge-extension under the overhang. With a good view of the tree and a raised lip to secure Cat's nest.

"But only for the summer," I decreed. *Or until Cat tires of bird-watching and finds a new way to torment me.*

A few days later, the worst happened. One of the nestlings fluttered onto the roof. Cat sat up. Strolled over, oh, so casual, and sniffed it. I was glad neither Martha nor Jamie was home to witness the nestling's end.

Cat ignored the parent birds dive-bombing his head. He picked up their baby by it's scrawny neck and stalked to the edge of the roof. Crouched. In one smooth leap, he cleared the hatchlings' nest, pivoted on the branch, and deposited the baby with its fellows. Then jumped back to our roof.

He curled up in his nest. Gave me one of his patented Cat-looks --- the one that says, "You were expecting something else?"

The next few weeks fell into a routine. Cat would watch the baby birds' flying lessons. And cat-nap in his nest under the eaves. I would watch Cat watch the nestlings. Pretend to be scanning the skies if Cat caught me watching him.

One morning, after being caught several times in quick succession, I lost sight of Cat. In the space between one breath and the next, he'd vanished. I scanned the roof and neighboring trees. *What if he'd fallen and was lying in the yard, hurt? Jamie and Martha would never forgive me.*

I set my binoculars on the window ledge and headed for the door. A marmalade streak rocketed past me. Swatted my binoculars. They crashed to the sidewalk below in a musical tinkle of splintering glass and plastic.

"Dammit, Cat." He was long gone. I headed downstairs for a broom and dust-pan.

I waited for Cat to abandon his nest once the hatchlings took to the skies. But he took to the roof almost every day and cat-napped in his nest. My sweaters were fur free for the first time in almost twelve years.

What he did next though, I swear, it was that bird's nest gave him the idea.

I happened to look out the window one afternoon and saw Cat at the edge of the roof. He sat back on his haunches --- a large, fluffy, marmalade gopher. And then, and this was the damndest thing ever, he launched himself towards the tree.

Thunk.

Cat hit a branch and grabbed on. Twigs crackled and snapped as he slid the rest of the way down. A few minutes later he was back on the roof. He stared over the edge. And did it again.

Three times, he climbed up and launched himself into the air.

The fourth time, he stared over the edge. Then stood up, stretched and walked away, tail in the air. He curled up in his nest with his back to the tree as if nothing had happened.

Next day, he wasn't in his nest. He wasn't in the kitchen when I came down for breakfast.

"I think Cat's finished with the bird's nest, Dad."

"Why do you say that, Jamie?"

"I saw just him pawing through the laundry basket for the sweater you're wearing."

I knew what that meant. I headed upstairs to retrieve the nest from our roof. And hollered at my long-suffering spouse, "Martha --- the cat's in my sweater drawer again.

• • •

The Impossible Passion of Persephone Jones

The familiar sounds of breakfast filled the sunny room: the muted gurgle of pouring tea, (*a dollop of milk, one lump of sugar*); the clink of spoon against china cup; the hypnotic *tick, tick* of the mantle clock in the parlor measuring out the morning; the rustle of fresh, crisp newsprint as each page's contents were examined, weighed and then placidly exchanged for the next.

"Mabel-dearest, where's the blue egg-cup?"

"Mmm?"

"The blue egg cup."

Mabel-dearest folded down one corner of the Home-Makers' section of the morning paper. She regarded her husband across the immaculately starched white tablecloth and raised an eyebrow. "Egg cup?"

Her husband, Horace Hennessey stared back, his round, pale-grey eyes made even rounder by the thick lenses of his steel-rimmed pince-nez. His mouth pursed, guppy-like, petulant.

"Egg cup?" she repeated, her pleasant smile only a little vague.

"Yes, Mable- dearest, do pay attention. The blue egg cup. With the pansies on it. My favourite. Where's the blue egg cup?"

A little crease appeared between Mabel's eyebrows. "Oh. Horace, the blue egg cup with the pansies on it. Oh, dear, I am so sorry. I dropped it while I was doing the washing up. I tried gluing it back together. It's in the rubbish bin. If you want I can get the pieces – " her voice trailed off.

Horace frowned. Removed his pince-nez and rubbed the bridge of his nose where the pads left a tiny, red dent on each side. "No, no. Best to just throw it away. No use in keeping something broken."

He set the pince-nez back in place and picked up his spoon. He tapped it against his egg, round and round the top of the shell. *Tap,*

tap, tap, tap. Sharp, precise little raps. The eggshell obliged, yielding with splintery crackles.

Hennessey turned his spoon and slipped the bowl into one of the cracks so it pierced the white and slid across the yolk, just kissing its smooth, yellow creaminess. Under his deft, firm pressure, the top lifted cleanly away, revealing the egg's molten center.

Horace carefully perused the toast "soldiers" lying in a row on his bread and butter plate. The slice of white bread had been lightly toasted, buttered evenly to every edge, not a single corner missed, and then carefully cut into exactly four equal fingers --- lengthwise, please, sideways would never do. "Soldiers", as his dear mother had always called them.

Mabel, dearest, bless her, called them "toast fingers." The name made him slightly squeamish, so he always pretended he hadn't heard what she said when she placed them on the table *"Your toast fingers are ready, Horace. Nice and hot, just the way you like them."*

Except he didn't really care for them hot, so he always let the soldiers cool while he drank his tea. His fingers hovered over the toast strips.

Mabel stared wide-eyed at his single-minded assault on the eggs' tender, white flesh, plunging each strip again and again into its creamy depths. Avidly savouring each yolk-drenched morsel.

Horace felt her gaze. He looked up. Their eyes met. He leaned across the table and fastened one strong hand in her short, dark curls. With the other, he ripped the freshly-starched cloth from the table, sending teapot, dishes and all crashing to the floor. He pulled Mabel towards him and buried his face in her neck. His fingers trailed down her cheek, strayed lower. He ripped her apron from around her waist and deftly hoisted her onto the table, his breath hot on her cheek. "Now, my saucy dove." he murmured --- "

"This one will do just as well, I expect."

"Pardon me?" Mabel blinked as reality reasserted itself.

Horace had finished eating and was admiring the little, yellow China cup which cradled the egg's plundered shell. "This egg cup. I rather like it. It's very – I don't know, cheerful. Don't you agree? I think it's my new favourite."

"Oh. Yes, of course, Horace-dear."

"Are you quite well, Mabel, dearest. You look a little flushed. I do hope you're not coming down with something."

Mabel raised a hand to her cheeks. "No, no I'm quite well, thank-you, Horace." She glanced at the newspaper lying open on her plate.

Horace's mouth pursed. He twitched the paper from Mabel's lax fingers and glanced through the story she's been reading. "Hmmph. As I suspected. A load of rubbish. Why they're allowed to print such nonsense, I'll never understand. And in the ladies' section. What's this country coming too?"

"I thought it was a rather good story, actually. It's by a new woman author."

Horace scowled so fiercely his eyebrows nearly met. "A woman? Preposterous. What editor worth his salt would publish some piece of fluff by a female?"

"It is the twentieth century, Horace. Women do write, you know."

"Yes, Mabel-dearest. They write poetry and literature. Not foolish romantic twaddle for the Friday Gazette." Horace settled his pince-nez more firmly. "Just listen to this...

'Oh, Roderigo.' Her creamy bosom heaved against her stays. 'My father has forbidden us to marry.' 'Then we shall run away together, my saucy dove.' The handsome, dark-haired Count Roderigo de la Vega leaned down. Her rosy lips parted. Roderigo claimed her tender mouth in an avid kiss – '

Good lord, I can scarcely bring myself to read it. It's preposterous. Impossible. Why it's almost smut." Horace's voice took on a familiar, hectoring tone. *His lecture-hall voice.* Mabel felt a tiny stab behind her right eye, the beginnings of a headache.

"And there's at least two, no three spelling mistakes. Shame on them. If an ordinary English

teacher like me can spot them, well, I ask you."
But, you don't really believe you're 'ordinary', do you, Horace?

He rattled the paper, scowling fiercely. "It escapes me how you can sit there, proudly complacent because this was written by a member of your sex. Just look at her name --- 'Persephone Jones?' Persephone Jones, indeed. Probably some fanciful nom-de-plume she made up so's not to embarrass her family. Good job she did, too, if you ask me."

Mabel-dearest bit back a sharp retort. *To think she'd once thought his pedantry was clever.* She'd even fondly imagined she and her college professor husband might collaborate. Mabel smiled and teased the paper from Horace's grasp. Smoothed it out.

"Actually, Horace-dear, there's a very nice recipe in this edition I thought I'd like to try for supper this evening. Of course, I'll need a small advance on the grocery money."

"How much?"

"Only a dollar or two, Horace-dear. I thought it would be nice to try something new. Perhaps, invite a few friends over to play whist after supper?"

"Oh, Mabel-dearest, it's Friday. Have you forgotten? We always have a nice baked ham with scalloped potatoes on Fridays, just as dear Mother used to make when she was alive. And then we listen to the New York Symphony Orchestra on the radio. Just as – "

" – just as we did while your dear mother was alive. Yes, of course, Horace-dear."

Mabel-dearest smiled and reached for the frozen picnic ham she'd set in the sink to thaw. "I'll just start the washing up, shall I? Off you go to work, now, Horace, dear." As Horace-dear turned for his hat and overcoat, Mabel swung the frozen ham as high as she could and brought it crashing down on Horace's head. He fell to the floor stone dead. As she rinsed off the ham and popped it into the oven, she wondered how long she should wait before calling the police to tell them dear Horace had been killed by a prowler who'd run off before she got a good look at him. Hmmm. Probably 'til the meat was cooked. Police work, especially chasing an murderous prowler, could make a man hungry, and she was sure they'd be glad of a nice ham sandwich.

"Well, I must be going. Are you sure you're alright, Mabel-dearest?"

Mabel blinked in the bright sunlight streaming through the cheerful, cherry-sprigged muslin draping her kitchen windows. "Yes, Horace-dear. Just a speck of something in my eye."

She quickly wiped her eyes on her apron and gave Horace a chaste peck on the cheek.

He smiled and patted his wife's shoulder, pleased with himself and his pleasantly predictable life. Pleased with the prospect of another day at the college, and looking forward to the benign routine of another Friday evening at home.

As the door closed behind Horace, Mabel gazed around her tidy kitchen. The freshly blacked range, the gleaming new ice-box, her spotlessly polished floors. Shining countertops. Everything neat and clean. Everything exactly in its place.

Mabel opened the pantry door and climbed to the top of her kitchen step stool. She reached behind the sparkling rows of preserves high on the top-most shelf to pull an old lard pail from the very back.

She checked the contents. Nearly a thousand dollars. *Not bad for a few pieces o* 'foolish, romantic twaddle.

She checked the contents. Nearly a thousand dollars. Not bad for a few pieces of impossible, foolish, romantic twaddle.

She unfolded the letter from Mills and Boon, and re-read it for the umpteenth time. 'Dear Miss Persephone Jones,' it began –

Mabel-dearest smiled. Replaced the publisher's offer letter in the lard pail. In another week or two, she'd have enough to leave. As dear Horace was so fond of saying, "No use keeping something broken." *Like their marriage.*

She wasn't sure where she'd go just yet. New York? Or New Orleans? In the meantime, her nest-egg was safe. It would never occur to dear Horace to open the pantry door for himself.

Humming the lively tune of a popular rag-time dance, Mabel cleared away the breakfast things and set a pan of water on the hob to heat for the washing up. As she tipped the shell bits into the dustbin, she stared at the little yellow cup remembering their first Christmas.

Horace's mother had gifted them with the set of twenty-four china egg cups. Hand-painted in different colours with dainty, little flowers.

"So her son would always have a clean egg cup for his breakfast," his mother said with a nasty gleam in her eye. *As if I didn't know how to wash dishes.*

Mabel tossed the egg cup in after the shells. It hit the side of the bin and shattered. *Favourite, indeed.* She giggled.

Two down, only twenty-two to go.

• • •

Here's To Star-Spangled Nights

Joelle huddled on the narrow, window-seat cushion and stared at the midnight sky. Mom would have her hide if she found her outta bed, but Joelle didn't care.

Mr. Dickey, the school librarian, had said there'd be a meteor shower, but this was so much grander than what Joelle had imagined.

"Shootin' stars," her dad called 'em. And so many --- a whole sky-full. *All those streaks of light pourin' down, faster'n faster.*

"What're you doin' up so late, Missy?"

Joelle nearly fell off her perch. "What're *you* doin' up?"

Her dad hitched a butt cheek on the window seat and pulled the chintz curtain aside. "Watchin' shootin' stars, same's you."

Joelle tucked her legs under her. The two stared through the wavy glass in companionable silence.

Joelle's mom padded, barefoot, up the stairs with a steaming mug. "Ha. Shoulda known I'd find the pair a' you moonin' out the window." She offered the mug to Joelle's dad.

He quirked a bushy brow at Joelle. "You want a sip, kiddo?"

Chamomile and fresh mint tickled her nose. The tea was thick with honey from their hives, just the way her dad liked it.

Joelle took another sip and passed the mug to her dad. "Someday, I'm gonna be an astronaut. I'll discover a new planet, an' when I come home they'll have a parade for me, an' a barbecue with fireworks, just like these shootin' stars."

"You can do anything you set your mind to, kiddo."

Joelle's mom snorted. "Neither one a' you'll be good for doin' much of anything, you don't get to bed soon." A chestnut curl flopped onto her mom's forehead. She tucked it under her headband.

Her dad laughed. "She gets it from you, Maggie-May --- wantin' to do somethin' big, make her mark." He pulled Joelle's mom onto his knee. "Just look at all those stars. A whole heaven's-worth a' them, lighting up the night. It feels kinda magical, doncha think?" He nuzzled the nape of her neck.

"You leave my neck all red with your scruffy whiskers, won't be nothin' magical about the talk in church come Sunday. What'll Mrs. Marley say."

"I expect Mrs. Marley will have quite a lot to say. She usually does."

Joelle's mom stifled a laugh. "Well, she is president of the Ladies' Afternoon Knitting Guild."

Joelle's dad chuckled. "Ah, Maggie-May, if only she knew what the preacher gets up to in his free time. What a tale she'd have to tell, then."

"It's a damn --- a darn good thing she doesn't, then, Preacher." Joelle's mom stood and swatted away the broad hand fondling her fanny. "Not in front of the k.i.d."

"The k.i.d. can hear you, Mom."

"Good, because if the k.i.d. isn't in bed in ten seconds – "

"But, Mom – "

"Don't be a whiny-baby. Nine – "

"Mr. Dickey says this won't happen again for years. This might be my only chance to see it."

"Yeah, Mom, it might be her only chance." Joelle's dad swept her mom into his arms and danced her into the hallway. His hand pistoned like a pump-jack in time to the goofy song he chanted about an old, drunk robber-lady.

Joelle grinned. Her parents made quite a pair.

Her dad, a big, burly, Viking bear, had hair stuck out like wheat straw and shovels for hands. But his touch was delicate as a surgeon's when bandaging a skinned knee or tending his beloved bees.

Her mother's petite frame and fine-boned features were a total misdirect. Margaret-Mary Pie was made of coiled-steel and tough as an old boot. Ex-army and proud of it.

Joelle's dad paused at the head of the stairs for a dramatic, movie-star dip and looked up. "I'll hold 'er off as long as I can, kiddo. Five minutes, tops."

He flung Joelle's mom over his shoulder and thundered downstairs. Moments later, their quiet laughter floated from the kitchen.

Joelle giggled and snuggled lower on the window seat. The streaks in the night sky beyond her window lessened, as the meteor-shower waned.

Joelle's eyelids drooped. Her head nodded. She jerked awake when her chin hit her chest. Once, twice – The third time, her eyes stayed shut.

She didn't waken when her dad carried her to bed. Nor when he tucked the flowered coverlet around her shoulder and kissed her forehead.

"Sleep well, kiddo. Dream about rocket ships and brave, new worlds."

He padded downstairs and flipped on the kitchen light. "Sitting alone in the dark, Maggie-May?"

Maggie smiled and held out her hand. "Give."

"Why, whatever do you mean, Margaret-Mary Pie."

"I felt the lump in your pocket, Mr. Pie."

"How d'you know I wasn't just glad to see you?"

Maggie's grin broadened. She waggled her fingers. "Gimme."

His eyes glinted as he leaned over her chair. He caught her lower lip between his teeth and nibbled, his warm breath minty from the tea. "Happy Meteor Shower, Mrs. Pie." He dropped a tiny crystal fish into her palm.

"Oh, Ben, it's beautiful." Maggie held the necklace up to the light. The little fish sparkled and bobbed on its silver chain.

"You like it? It makes rainbows in the sunlight."

"I love it --- but – " Maggie nodded to the stoop-shouldered giant of a refrigerator crouched at the end of the counter.

Entire schools of fish magnets cavorted across its heavy white door.

Glass fish, wooden fish, China fish, flat woven-straw fish; a rainbow of red, blue, green, and yellow fish; lavender and purple and pink fish; striped fish; spotted fish; spiny fish; miniature Minnows and Perch and Bass. Elegant fish with gilded scales. Flying fish. Engraved fish. Articulated fish with flapping tails. Fish with bulging eyes and sparkling bubbles rising from their lips.

"I thought it'd be a change from magnets."

Maggie smiled. "I love my fish magnets." She pointed to a red and blue paper-mâché trout, dead-center in the swirling schools. "Remember?"

Ben knelt beside her chair and fastened the silver chain 'round her neck. "How could I forget. You were the prettiest girl at the Fourth of July picnic, and I had to do something to keep you away from Roger Cunningham at the Kissing Booth." He leveled a stern finger at her nose. "Roger had his eye on you. It was fish or cut bait."

Maggie laughed. "I knew you cheated. You told those nice ladies behind the curtain at the 'Wishing Well' to tie that trout on my fishing pole, didn't you? Instead of a heart pin or their homemade chocolates."

"Yes, they were nice ladies." Ben nuzzled her cheek. "What can I say? You liked the fish. I didn't want you to be disappointed. A pastor should have some pull at his church's booth."

Maggie fingered the little, crystal fish. "Do you really think Joelle will become an astronaut, Ben?"

"Well, she's only ten. She could change her mind again. Last month she was set on being a ballerina, or joining the Marines." He grinned. "I don't believe a dance studio's been created yet could handle Joelle, but she'd make one fine Marine."

"Hoo-rah."

"Ya know, Maggs, I never planned to be a pastor. Not when I was her age. I was happy just working at Grandad's honey farm. But here I am."

Maggie chuckled. "Pastor Pie, the beekeepin' preacher, purveyor of fine fish magnets."

"You love your fish magnets."

"I do." Maggie linked her arm through his. "Let's go snuggle on the porch swing and watch the shooting stars. See if we can scandalize the neighbors."

Ben waggled his eyebrows and flashed a wicked grin.

"C'mon, Romeo." Still laughing, Maggie led him into the star-spangled night.

• • •

The Stork Cometh: A Love Story

Two souls brought together by a dirty diaper

Brian scowled at the squalling infant in the hobo-sling swaddling bag. The sharp, acrid odor arising from the business end (*as opposed to the 'bottle end'*) was truly an appalling stench. Worthy of any sewer rat.

He was eternally amazed by how one tiny, heaven-sent morsel of life could produce so much noise and such outrageous stinks. *The mind boggles.*

Brian laid the wee mite on her back on the park bench, shushing and singing bits of nonsense in a soft, lullaby-voice. This did nothing to stem the flow of outraged suffering. If anything, the child's cries grew louder.

He gingerly unwrapped the dainty, hand-crocheted pink blanket and unsnapped the tiny, flower-sprigged onesie. His eyes watered at the pungent smell.

Brian blinked hard, trying not to gag. "I can do this," he muttered.

He fished in his carry-all for lotion, wipes and a fresh diaper. Then, he carefully removed the offending article and stuffed it into a plastic-lined pouch for later disposal.

"Now, to wipe you all clean..."

The tiny girl squirmed and wiggled, kicking her legs at the indignity, hollering even more loudly. Brian wished for the umpteenth time babies came with a volume control.

Ignoring her screams, he folded the fresh, soft, cloth diaper and slid it under her little bottom. But the over-sized, pink, plastic-headed safety pins proved beyond him. He stabbed himself three times before he finally fastened one side, only to find she'd peed in the clean diaper.

All he could do was to unpin it, fold a new one and try again --- with the same result.

After his second attempt, Brian sat for a moment, re-grouping.

He gazed around the tranquil little park. Everywhere he looked, mothers were enjoying the fresh spring air. Rocking their babies in prams, or chatting together on one of the benches while their toddlers clambered on the jungle gym, or played in the sand box.

"Don't eat that, Robby --- that's dirty! No. Yucky!"

As far as Brian could tell, Robby thought the sand was pretty tasty. He managed to stuff a mitt-full into his mouth before his mother could grab him.

Brian noticed a few dads huddled together, trying hard to look like they weren't checking out the moms, while their various, also-male offspring tussled over a soccer ball.

"You look like you could use a hand." A young woman perched beside Brian on the park bench, deftly pinned the diaper in place, and picked up the grizzling baby.

"Well, aren't you the precious little one," she crooned. "Look at you. Yes. You are. You are a precious little girl."

She cradled the infant in one arm and slipped her into a fresh, floral-sprigged onesie. Then with the ease of long practice, she popped the infant back into the hobo-sling, tucking the pink blanket tenderly around her.

The baby gurgled and waved her tiny fists.

Brian was impressed. "You certainly have a way with little people."

The young woman's dark eyes twinkled. "I have six brothers and sisters, all younger. You don't forget how after helping with that many." She ran a long-fingered, cafe-au-lait hand over her intricately braided corn-rows.

She had the most amazing hair Brian had ever seen. Where the braids ended near the back of her beautifully-shaped head, a halo of shining, crinkly curls flowed free in a glorious riot of ebony, chestnut, and amber, streaked through with copper and tawny gold.

He suddenly realized he was staring. He cleared his throat. "Thanks again for your help with the diaper. I was almost ready to give up."

The young woman smiled, showing perfect, white teeth. "I'm Koneesha."

"Sorry, where are my manners? I'm Brian."

"Nice to meet you, Brian."

Brian ducked his head. "Nice to meet you, too, Koneesha."

The baby hiccupped. Brian could tell she was working herself up to another yell-fest.

"Well, I'd better get going again," he said. "Before she does."

The baby let out a few experimental squawks, then settled into a steady rhythm.

Koneesha smiled again. "Too late." She raised her voice over the baby's clamor. "I'm here most mornings, watching my nephew." She nodded towards a little guy in a Spider Man tee-shirt hanging from the top rung of the monkey bars. "If he doesn't kill himself."

Right on cue, her nephew slipped. Hanging by one hand, hollering for help. Koneesha laughed. "Maybe you'll stop by another time?"

Brian thought she had a wonderful laugh. "Well, um, yes. Yes. I could stop by --- another time."

"Good. I'll look forward to that." Koneesha trotted off to rescue her nephew.

Brian wondered, just for an instant, what might be if things were different. It was hard enough to meet someone, let alone someone as caring and lovely as Koneesha. And she did seem to like him, too.

But with his schedule --- on call almost twenty-four seven. *Still, if things were different* –

Brian sighed. *Onward.*

He shook out his magnificent pinions and stretched them to their full length. Slid his long, strong beak through the knotted hobo-sling holding the still-squalling infant. "You'll be home soon, 'precious little one'," he said.

He flexed his long slim legs and sprang aloft, beating his way skyward with strong, steady strokes.

As he flapped away in search of Nineteen-Twenty-Three Lamont Drive where his precious bundle's expectant parents waited, he realized how very much he was looking forward to seeing Koneesha again.

To think they'd met, because of a dirty diaper. Funny old world. In the meantime, though, he had a job to do. And a company slogan to uphold:

"Storks Unlimited --- Leave Your Difficult Deliveries To Us"

"Ah, well," he thought. "A *job's a job. Still, life was so much simpler when people just found their babies under a leaf in the cabbage patch.*"

• • •

Summer Lightning

The old ones tell a story. A youth will come, born of the storm. A maid will take him to her for a single year. And the storm will keep its promise and make fruitful the thirsty land. And the maid will keep her promise. Blood for blood, life for a life. Sealed by the lightning.

I jerked awake, my heart pounding, mouth dry, muscles bow-taut. The dream – fear clawed my throat. *Blood for blood, life for a life.* A year together in exchange for the rain. A promise I'd always kept. Always. *'Til, twenty years ago.* A distant rumble warned of the approaching storm. *No, no – not yet.* But my heart knew and so did the storm.

Beside me, Michael stirred and muttered in his sleep. I lay beside him, my body still as death, longing for the comfort of his arms. For the warm silk of his skin on mine, heart to heart, legs entwined. I ached to rest my head in the perfect hollow where his strong, wind-burned neck met his shoulder. To pretend this was just another night.

Instead, I held my breath 'til he settled, then slid out of bed and padded across the room.

The sprigged muslin curtains fluttered in the rising breeze. Chilled, I rubbed my arms and wondered if I should close the window. Lightning flared low on the horizon, eerie greenish streaks momentarily linking the parched earth to the roiling thunderheads.

The wind caught my hair and dragged it free of its ties. I raked a hand through the silver-threaded chestnut waves to snag the narrow blue ribbon fluttering at my nape, but the wind whipped it away. As I smoothed the unruly tangle back from my forehead, wiry silver strands crackled and clung. Michael had laughed with delight the first time he ran his fingers through my lightning-charged halo, the chestnut curls clinging round his hand.

Images of our beginning tumbled through my mind. My young love cradling a new-born foal, his face alight with wonder. The first time he tasted spring rain, and lay with me under the stars – and still, the fever rush when our eyes meet. In twenty years, that hasn't changed. And in twenty years, I've forgotten nothing of our days. Or our nights. I cannot forget. It's my only gift now – remembering.

Now, Michael's hands bear the scars of twenty years unrelenting toil, coaxing tender green shoots from the dying land. *His hands bring life. Mine, only death.*

Death for the world.

Death for him.

I knew, without checking the mirror, new lines had formed by my eyes. Laugh lines? Nothing much to laugh about, now.

Once, there was summer wine, dew-fresh grass beneath bare feet, wild roses and strawberries. Autumn, crisp with scarlet and gold leaves fluttering, tumbling, crunching underfoot. The tang of frost-kissed apples spiced with cinnamon. Long winter nights by the fire. Warm woollen blankets. Hot cocoa and mulled wine, sweet on the tongue.

The huge limbs of the giant oak in the yard below groaned and swayed. Struck by lightning in the last big storm, twenty years ago, one side of the tree'd been sheared away as if by a giant's knife.

Miraculous and stubborn, the tree survived. Dead at its core, the hollow oak still managed to send out green shoots and new leaves each spring and spread its remaining branches to offer welcome shade from the blast furnace of our summer.

And, like the venerable oak, our town managed to cling to life. Surviving somehow on the trickle of water the windmills coaxed to the surface. But the twenty-year drought was winning, killing us off one farm at a time, as one family after another piled their life in a truck-box and fled. Leaving silent, hollow-eyed children with swollen bellies and desiccated twig-limbs to clutch their despairing parents' hands and stare after departing friends from behind dust-smeared windows.

A sudden gust rattled the leaves on the aspen poplars by the barn. They seemed to be whispering to each other, "Maybe tonight – maybe this time?"

I shivered and reached for the sash to close the window.

"You had the dream again."

I jumped. *Dammit*. I turned from the storm outside to face the one within.

Michael leaned on his elbow, his dark hair tousled from sleep. His beautiful hazel eyes, usually so sunny, flashed amber fire. "Didn't you?"

I couldn't lie. I nodded.

Thunder crashed again, louder, closer. Lightning flickered and danced across the brazen sky. And I could see an answering storm rising in Michael's eyes. His brow furrowed, jaw stubborn-set.

Michael swung long legs over the side of the bed and wrapped the sheet, toga-like, around his waist. "It's time." *No – don't say that. I'm not ready.*

He strode across the room, tall and lithe, his curly hair brushing the steep-pitched ceiling. He sank onto the window seat and stared out at the heart of the storm. Then he grasped my arms; pulled me down beside him. I could feel the heat of him through the sheet. Lost in thought, his thumb idly traced the contour of my cheek as he had done so often in the soft silence after love. Then, his eyes searched mine.

"I know you had the dream again. It's time."

It's well past time — twenty years past.

Thunder rattled the window-frame. *Close it. Don't look.* I covered my face with my hands to blot out the storm, to hold back the unshed tears burning my eyes. Fighting to deny the awful truth.

Lightning cracked, so near the house, I saw the glare of its spiking fire through my tight-squeezed eyelids. *Please, I'm not ready. I can't – I can't breathe.*

"It's time." Michael's steel-edged command cut through the storm's clamour.

I stared, after twenty years finally seeing him. My beautiful love. *He knows. He's always known. Even before I told him my dream.*

Salt-drops rolled down my cheeks, bitter on my tongue. I slid to my knees, sobbing, and wrapped my arms around his legs. The words ripped from my heart. "Please. I can't. I can't do it again."

Twenty years I'd had with Michael. Twenty precious, stolen years and not one drop of rain had fallen. Still, I couldn't give him up. *I won't – not again.* Everything could die. I wanted everything to die. Then I would die too, and it would be over.

Michael raised me from the floor. Brushed my forehead with his lips, soft as a butterfly's wing. Cradled me against his chest, his breath warm in my hair. Gradually my racing heart slowed. Matched his heart's steady rhythm.

"I stayed for you," he whispered.

"But – " I tilted my head back. Gazed at his face, taut with an expression I couldn't quite read.

His generous mouth twitched. "You are not the only one who loves."

"You were supposed to go back twenty years ago." My cheeks burned. "I couldn't give you up."

Michael looked away. "You couldn't help but love me. The storm made me for you."

My heart gave a painful jerk. "The storm – made you?"

Michael's hazel eyes returned to mine, glowing with the light of the summer sun. "Yes. The storm made me – and the storm is me. But it did not know I would want to stay."

I pulled away, chilled to my core. *His words echoed in my head –'The storm made me, the storm made me.'* But, though my mind heard his words, my heart denied them.

"No – no. You're flesh and blood. A man, the same as any man." *But not the same, never the same, for you are my only beloved.* "You cried for joy the first time you heard a mockingbird's song. You always leave your socks under the bed. You – The storm stole you from some grieving mother –"

"No, my love." Michael's smile was tinged with sadness. "I am flesh and blood and bone and sinew. My heart yearns and breaks like yours. But I am born of the storm. And to the storm I must return. And you, Amiah, beloved –" His hand cupped my cheek. "You are the keeper of the promise."

His words pierced my soul. I wanted to hurt him as he was hurting me. "You're not the first." My voice sounded cold, distant – *My bones are ice. I am hollowed out and my heart is turned to stone.*

He nodded. "Nor will I be the last. But I will always be."

A stubborn flicker of hope stirred, refused to be stilled. "What do you mean, 'I will always be' – will you come back? Is it always you who comes back?"

Michael shook his head. "No, beloved. We can come only once. But the storm –"

"No." I wrenched away. "I don't want the storm, I want you."

Michael grabbed my arms and tried to pull me close. I screamed and slammed my fists into his chest again and again, my fury matching the storm.

A sheet of lightning flashed across the sky, enveloping us in its white-hot glare. And in an instant, we were standing under the oak tree.

 It was my dream. Michael, twenty years ago, beautiful in his youth and strength. A young David facing Goliath, shining white against the oak tree in the dark heart of the storm.

I screamed his name, my cry barely audible over the shrieking wind.

The knife gleamed in my hand, raised high. "No – take me – "
But there was no bargaining with the storm. The lightning claimed the knife, blazed a trail of fire towards my love. Then, a blinding flare.

Michael cried out in agony as the light consumed him. His skin flamed and blackened, shredded away in a flurry of grey flakes borne on the wind. His bones glowed white, incandescent, then crumbled to dust. The stench of burnt-offering hung in the air.

As the cold rain began to fall, soaking the scorched, thirsty ground, I turned towards the white clapboard farmhouse, in my mouth the taste of ashes, my body heavy as death. I knew, without looking, my hair was dark again, my face unlined.

"Is it you?" His voice was so young.

Not again. I can't do it again.

A blackened, barren landscape filled my mind. No farms, no life, no suffering children. I opened my arms and welcomed the desolation. I was fading, dissolving. And he spoke again –

"Are you the one?"

Everything or nothing. That was my choice.

For one frozen moment, life and breath and sense stopped.

Don't look back. But all the pain to come could not quench the whisper of hope rising in my breast – a tiny, fluttering bird.

I turned.

Standing where the blasted tree had been, a sturdy sapling raised its leafy head. And under the tree, a beautiful youth with autumn hair and lightning in his golden eyes.

"Are you the one?" he asked again.

My throat closed. I nodded.

He held out his hand. Long-fingered, beautiful. Unmarked by this life.

I knew he wasn't Michael. Knew he couldn't be – still I searched his eyes, trying to surprise some small piece of my lost love in those golden depths.

He cocked his head to one side. "Do you know me?"

Nothing – there was nothing of Michael in these eyes. I closed my eyes against the prick of bitter tears.

Warm fingers stole into mine. He took my hand in both of his and placed it on his chest. And in the measured beat of his heart, I heard the echo of Michael's voice "My heart yearns and breaks like yours. It loves as deep and long as yours."

I saw the coming year. Dancing under the grape arbor in the morning mist, our bodies pressed close in the perfect harmony of lovers. Sharing a warm, crusty, loaf fresh from the oven, thick-slathered with butter and black-berry jam. Sugar cookies cooling on the kitchen sill. Heads together of a long winter's eve by the fire as we searched out pieces of a "Where's Waldo" jigsaw puzzle. Laughing at our lop-sided snowmen 'til our bellies ached and carolling off-key to the cat family in the barn, fluffy grey mites with pale pink noses curled, trusting, in our mittened hands.

I opened my eyes. Breathed deep of the cooling air. *Life will go on. We will go on.*

"I know you," I said.

He smiled like the sun coming out, and my heart shattered in a million pieces. For I knew I would love him. And when our year was done, I would bring him to the oak tree and return him to the storm. The parched land would live again. And my heart would die with each new love.

The old ones tell a story. A youth will come, born of the storm. A maid will take him to her for a single year. And the storm will keep its promise and make fruitful the thirsty land. And the maid will keep her promise. Blood for blood, life for a life. Sealed by the lightning.

• • •

All The Time In The World

"This is a test --- it is only a test. If it had been an actual life, you would have received further instructions on where to go and what to do."

The words scrolled across the bottom of the screen. The annoying two-tone, warning signal blared again. Wee-ooh, wee-ooh, wee-ooh. Then the screen flashed and the scrolling banner reappeared.

"Hey, Maddie has the Wi-Fi gone crazy?"

Wee-ooh, wee-ooh, wee-ooh.

"Shit. Now my phone's doing it." Jackson grabbed his cell and swiped down for notifications. He glanced up as Maddie hurried in, phone in hand. "I thought it might be an amber alert but there's nothing."

"What's with the TV?"

"I know, isn't that a weird message?"

Maddie tucked a vagrant blonde strand behind her ear and frowned. "It's just another annoying test. But those shadow thingies are weird."

Jackson stared.

The scrolling ticker-tape now read: "This is a test of the Emergency Broadcast System. If this had been an actual emergency you would have been given instructions on where to go."

Behind the words, silhouetted against glowing, blue static, a pair of dark figures jumped up and down and waved their arms.

"What on earth?" Maddie reached towards the screen.

"Don't touch it." Jackson grabbed her hand. "Please."

Maddie drew back. But a tiny smile pulled at the corner of her lips. "Jackson, you're not afraid of shadows are you?"

"No, I just... I... maybe?"

"Oh, Jacks, it's your dream, isn't it? The one you wrote about in your novel, "What Darkness Waits in The Shadows?"

Jackson swallowed hard. Nodded.

"Babe, your agent loved it. Your publisher loved it. You scared over a million readers into sleeping with the lights on. But it's just a story. The shadows aren't real."

His head hurt. Blood pounded in his ears. A voice in his head repeated, "*Stop, Maddie. Please, stop.*"

Maddie placed her palm on Jackson's chest. "Breathe with me. Slow, deep breaths."

"*Please stop, Maddie. Please, stop Maddie. Stop Maddie. STOP MADDIE.*"

Jackson forced his fists to unclench. Drew a deep, shuddering breath. Then another. The pain in his head eased.

"There you are." Maddie brushed her lips against his. Ruffled his short, dark curls. "Better?"

"What would I do without you?" He slipped an arm round her waist.

"Finish your next best-seller?" Laughing, Maddie pointed at the TV. "Babe, there's nothing to be afraid of."

The shadows in the blue static waved, frantic. A surge of panic drove Jackson forward. "Maddie, stop."

She smiled at him as her finger touched the screen.

A white-hot spark leapt from TV. Enveloped her in its brilliant glare. The last thing Jackson saw was two shadows, his and Maddie's, burnt into the wall behind the television.

Then the universe blinked out.

• • •

The little boy stared at the shadow in the pond. The sun was low behind him, making the shadow long and pointy. His mother was calling. But she was far away. The whispery voice in his head almost drowned her out.

"It's your shadow, Jackson. Don't be afraid. Touch it."

"I'm not s'posed ta play in the water. I hafta stay nice for Grandma."

"Just one finger, Jackson. You'll still be nice for Grandma."

"I'm not s'posed ta talk to strangers." The boy's voice quavered.

"It's alright, Jackson. I'm not a stranger. I'm 'Friend'. We talk every night, before you fall asleep."

"Friend?"

"That's right. Touch your shadow. You'll remember, then."

The boy leaned over the shallow water. Folded his hand into a fist and stuck out his index finger. A bright blue spark fizzed up his arm.

"Ow." He stuck his finger in his mouth. "Shit. You didn't tell me it'd hurt, jerk-off." Grown-up Jackson in the body of a seven-year-old wearing Penguin-print overalls.

"If I'd told you, you wouldn't have done it. Now, remember, keep it simple, Jackson. Make sure you meet Maddie. She's the key."

"My head hurts. You shoved a lotta stuff in there. I have to stop her touching the shadows, right?" He stopped mid-flow. "You'll be there with me."

"No, Jackson. We talked about this. We'll help as much as we can, but it'll feel like an urge, an

*inner prompting. You'll have to trust your
instincts."*

"When did we talk about this?"

"The last time."

"Last time?"

"And the time before that."

"How many times have we done this?"

"In my lifetime, this will be your third rewind."

"My third --- rewind? In your lifetime. Why
don't I remember?"

*"It fades very quickly, Jackson. And some
things never come back. But the important parts
will stay as impulses --- a driving force in your life."*

Friend paused, gauging Jackson's reaction. *"I
am your fifth 'Friend', Jackson. You've been reset
twice in my tenure. This time we took you back
to age seven to stay outside the anomaly. It
grows with each reset, so we have to go back a
bit further every time. If it gets too big --- "*

"I'll be too young to understand?"

*"You won't be born yet. And if that happens,
your reality collapses."*

Jackson paled. "My reality?"

Friend was silent. Then, "Everyone's reality."

Jackson crumpled to his knees. "I think I'm gonna puke."

"Don't puke. You have to stay clean for Grandma."

"Fuck Grandma." Jackson rocked back on his heels and buried his face in his hands. "Four other Friends?" He did the math. "Shit --- we've been at this for almost five hundred years?"

"Yes."

"And I still haven't got it right?"

"Jackson..."

"You gotta get somebody else." Tears welled up. "Please. What if I screw up again?"

"Jackson..."

Jackson scrubbed his sleeve across his face. "Shit. We've talked about this before, too, haven't we?"

"Jack-son." His mom's voice called from farther down the path. "Where are you?"

"Wait, I'll tell Mom. Right now, before I forget. She'll remember it for me." He raced down the path and ran head-long into his mother. "Oof!"

She set him back on his feet and cupped his tear-stained cheeks between her palms. "Don't cry, sweet boy. I've got you now."

"Mama, the shadows are --- " Jackson frowned. It was important, he was sure. "The shadows..."

She wrapped her arms around the little boy. "You're safe, Jackson. The shadows can't get you. Mama's here."

Jackson snuggled into her warmth. There was something he needed to tell her... something about the shadows. But he was so tired. He rested his head on his mother's shoulder and listened to her humming a lullaby as she carried him down the path towards home.

As he drifted off, a name fluttered to the surface. "Maddie," he murmured. "...hurry, Mama."

His mother kissed his dark curls. "You can tell me about Maddie in the morning. There's no rush, sweet boy. We have all the time in the world."

• • •

Dream Weaver

The shuttle flies back and forth across the warp. Ticking, clicking, untiring, unceasing it weaves the fabric of life on the Loom of Time. The blind muse dips her hand into the basket at her feet and gathers threads for the ever-changing tapestry.

The cosmos wheels and spins around her, in perfect harmony with her measured beat and flow. The filmy, star-kissed fabric weightless yet heavy with all the cares of the world falls across her thighs.

She runs her hand over it. Feels the shift and play of each strand. She catches the end of a single thread.

Her shuttle stills its rhythmic flight as she untangles the strand from its sisters and rolls it between her palms.

It seems ordinary. Unremarkable. It doesn't shine with flecks of gold like the strands next to it.

If anything, it makes those nearby all the brighter for its plainness. Yet, there's a hidden richness –

The muse rethreads the strand. "Let us see how your light will shine, little one."

Zzzz, click. Clackety-clack, thunk. Zzzz, click. Clackety-clack, thunk. The hypnotic rhythm of shuttle and loom filled the quiet loft. Marking the hours in time with the tick-tock of the ancient grandfather clock in the downstairs parlor.

Wooden, honeycomb shelves lined both sides of the narrow, sun-dappled room. A rainbow of hand-dyed skeins crammed every nook.

A huge half-circle window took up the gable-end wall. Its center, a four-paned window-within-a-window, stood wide to catch the fitful spring breeze. A comfy, wing-back chair and matching footstool squatted nearby. With a small, gate-leg table in easy reach, perfect for a mug of tea and a good book.

A heavy, oak, four-poster loom commanded the center of the room. Its ancient uprights worn satin-smooth by the generations of weavers who'd served as custodians of the Conklin loom. Five-times-great Uncle Elias Conklin had it built for his new bride. Since then, it'd passed from mother to daughter, down to its current guardian, Anna-May Conklin.

She smiled as she worked the treadles with her bare feet. "*Some day, this old beauty will go to one a' my girls.*"

The front door crashed open. School shoes clattered onto the boot-rack. Dire threats rang through the downstairs entry. Followed by the rush of bare feet up the stairs and blood-curdling rebuttals. Bedroom doors slammed.

Anna-May sighed. "*If they don't kill each other first.*" She wondered which child would arrive first for a motherly consult.

Her eldest, Serena Joy, named for both grandmothers, was anything but serene. Or joyful. At eleven, she was intense and brooding. Until her awkward, coltish bundle of elbows and knees transformed to ethereal grace with the lilt of any tune.

Or little Prue — Elizabeth Prudence. Now seven, her bright butterfly was determined to outgrow her baby-name 'Lilli-bit'. She insisted on Prudence or Prue. There were already three

'Elizabeths' in her grade at school and Prue, the budding artist, was a one-of-a-kind spirit.

But it was Anna-May's middle child who made her silent way to the loft. Nine-going-on-forty, June — *just June, no middle name, thank you* — was inclined to shyness and self-doubt.

"God don't make mistakes. Ain't that right, Mama?"

"Yes, indeed, sweet girl. Though it c'n take us mere mortals a while to figure out exac'ly what God intended. Why d'you ask, Junie-bug?"

Hot tears spilled down the little girl's cheeks. " 'Cuz I can't dance like Sissie, an' I'll never be pretty as Prue, or paint half so good… I think God put me in the wrong family."

Anna-May's shuttle stilled. She regarded her daughter's tragic face. "You think so, do you?"

June's gaze fell. She rubbed one foot against the back of her other leg. "I got eyes, Mama."

"Ahh."

Anna-May pulled the little girl onto her lap. "Help me with this. Here, take the shuttle and put it in there. Now, give it a push. Not too hard. Perfect. Now, I'll catch it and push it back to you. That's it."

The easy rhythm of catch and push soon claimed the child's attention.

"June, can I tell you something I've never told anyone before?"

The little girl nodded.

"When I was about your age, Grammy Alice told me, 'Anna-May, you're just like me. I was never a pretty girl. And you won't be either, But when you're older, you'll be a handsome woman. And I promise, you'll be your own woman.' " Anna-May shook her head. "Until that moment, I believed one day I would be pretty."

June's hand paused, the shuttle's rhythm interrupted. "But you are pretty, Mama. Grammy was mean to say that."

"Bless you, darlin'." Anna-May kissed the top of her daughter's head. "Grammy didn't intend to be unkind. She knew I would grow into my looks. Mostly, though, she wanted me to be myself. Not waste my days yearning after what the rest of the world valued. But she broke a little piece of my heart that day. And it took years to mend."

June picked at a thread. "How did you mend it, Mama?"

"By finding what I love to do. And doing it as hard as I could."

"Like when Sissie dances?"

Anna-May smiled at her clever daughter. "Yes. And the way Lilli-bit paints."

The little girl giggled. "You mean Prue." The shuttle resumed its schussing traverse across the threaded warp.

"Yes, 'Prue'. And the way you write stories."

June absorbed that idea. "Can we add a different color?"

"If it fits our story, of course."

"What story?"

"Why, the story we're making right now. We choose the colors, where each is placed… and the finished cloth will tell our story. The same way you tell a story by weaving words together."

June dipped into the basket of skeins. "Can we put this red one here?"

"Oh, my, that's a bright one. Who is that?"

"It's Sissy. See? With the yellow — that's her sunflower dress. She's dancing."

"Of course. It's exactly like her."

Zzzz, click. Clackety-clack, thunk. Zzzz, click. Clackety-clack, thunk. The hypnotic rhythm filled the quiet loft. Heads together, mother and daughter wove their story on the family loom. The murmur of their voices marked the hours in time with the tick-tock of the ancient grandfather clock in the downstairs parlor.

And the cosmos wheels and spins around them, in perfect harmony with their measured beat and flow.

• • •

The Lunchbox

School Days

Andy Anderson skipped down the back lane on his way to school, his well-worn Buster Browns raised puffs of dust in the uneven, rutted gravel. One fist clutched tight round the handle of his precious new lunchbox while the theme from his favorite TV show bubbled through his mind,

Crash. The little boy hit the ground, sharp gravel biting into bare knees and tender palms. His lunchbox clattered against a wooden fence post and skittered into the middle of the lane. Blinking back tears, Andy clambered to his feet, picking bits of dirt and crushed rock from bloody weals while his new lunchbox vanished up the lane in the hands of his school-playground tormentor, Bobby Burroughs.

Bobby's crowing laugh floated back to Andy on the crisp morning air.

Andy brushed the grime from the front of his checkered, short-sleeved shirt, and fingered the rip in the hem of his knee-length pants, relieved he hadn't been wearing his new sweater with the brown leatherette trim. Mom woulda been plenty mad if he'd got that dirty on the first day of school.

"Oh, sweetie, not the sweater, too," she'd said when he marched downstairs, so proud in his new clothes. "Let's save it for school pictures day."

Andy didn't want to disappoint his mom so he'd agreed, but he'd planned to wait 'til she left for work, then let himself in with his key and sneak back upstairs for it. Mom didn't get off shift 'til way after he got home from school so he'd have time to put the sweater back in his drawer.

Now, though, he was glad he'd chickened out. He didn't like lying to his mom. Even the little, needful lies he would tell when she'd ask if he'd been lonely by himself after school, or if the meatloaf was okay. Andy wasn't a good liar. His ears turned pink and his eyes would go all squinty. Then he'd blink and look away.

But his mom would just smile and say, "Are you sure, sweetie?"

Andy would duck his head so she couldn't see his face and tell her, "No, I just read my comics." Or, "Meatloaf's fine tonight, Mom." And add another glob of ketchup or take a big gulp of milk to wash it down.

Mom had looked real nice this morning in her smart navy car coat and new navy straw hat. Not that she didn't usually look nice with her dark brown eyes and soft wavy hair in a neat bun. Andy thought she was pretty. Every bit as pretty as the Kraft Dinner mom in the magazines. But this morning had been special -- she was going to be interviewed to be Head Teller at the bank. She'd worked there as long as Andy could remember. Since before his dad went overseas. Before his plane crashed and he never came home.

Andy had been too little then to remember much of their old life. But his mom had showed him her photo albums from before. Sometimes she would pull out the projector on a Saturday night and they'd watch the grainy home movies his dad had made of their trips.

To the beach, to the Arizona dessert one year. To the California coast to see the giant redwoods. Andy and his mom would eat popcorn and she'd tell stories about their travels, Where they'd stayed, what she and his Dad had talked about.

They always ended with the reel of his dad holding Baby Andy in his christening gown and lace bonnet, then waving from a train, in his airman's uniform.

And his mom always said, "Doesn't your dad look handsome in his uniform? Such a dashing pilot."

Andy wasn't sure what 'dashing' meant but he'd nod anyway.

The movie was short, which Andy figured was a good thing, because it always made his mom sad. Then she would dry her eyes and hug Andy extra hard, and they'd have vanilla ice cream with chocolate sauce.

Andy sighed. He wondered how he was going to tell his mom about the lunch box. He'd begged and pestered her for months. Finally they'd struck a bargain. And he'd done his level best.

"Sweetie, you know the deal we made," his mom had said. "You can buy the lunch box when you've saved up enough for it."

"But I've saved my whole allowance, Mom. I haven't bought a single comic all year."

Andy's mother smiled. She knew how much her boy loved his comics.

"But even with last year's birthday and Christmas money from Auntie Babs, I only have six-fifty."

Andy had stared at the ad in the back of last year's Superman Special Issue. "Get your official Roy Rogers lunch box with matching Thermos. Only eight dollars and eighty-seven cents, including postage." Might as well have been eight-million.

Then, a miracle happened. A cardboard box addressed to him arrived just before his eighth birthday and the start of the new school year. Andy ripped it open and gasped, goggle-eyed.

"Mom -- it's the lunch box!" He'd flung his arms around her neck, lunchbox in hand. "Thanks."

Andy's mother had smiled. "Well, you only turn eight once," she'd said.

Andy sighed and blew on his stinging palms. His mom had made up the extra he'd needed. Most likely out of her lunch money. And now his cherished lunch box was gone.

Head hanging, he trudged the length of the lane and turned onto the busy street leading to his school. Mr. Darnley, the crossing guard was at his post same as last year. Every June he swore it'd be his last, but every fall he was back on the sidewalk, sign in hand, keeping 'his kids' safe. His peaked cap a bit sideways on his bushy white hair, horn-rim glasses low on his nose.

He waved at Andy. "Get a wiggle on, Sonny. Cars won't wait all mornin'."

All the boys were "Sonny" to Mr. Darnley. All the girls were "Missie." Anyone over the age of a school girl was "Missus." Andy had never heard Mr. Darnley speak to a man. Prob'ly he thought they were old enough to cross on their own.

Andy hurried over the crosswalk and up the wide stone steps leading to the school's main foyer. His shoes squeaked on the polished green floor tiles. Andy heard a snicker and glanced over. Three older boys were slouched on the bench outside the main office.

Already? Andy wondered what they'd done so early on the first day to earn a seat there. He didn't wonder for long, though. He was more concerned about what he was going to have for lunch. He supposed he could use his milk money for a bowl of soup and a bun. But first, he had to get through assembly without running into Bobby Burroughs. Again.

No such luck.

The first person he saw in the crowded auditorium, blocking the way to the long row where the rest of the Grade Twos waited, was Bobby.

"Where's my lunchbox." Andy blurted out the question before he had time to consider what might happen.

Bobby turned. Stared down his snub nose at the younger, smaller boy and frowned.

"What lunch box, twerp?"

"My new Roy Rogers lunch box. You took it when you pushed me down in the lane."

"You seen me take it, didja, twerp."

"No, but you pushed me and -- and I saw you running away."

"You saw me running away. With your Roy Rogers lunch box? And just what would I want with a baby's cowboy lunch box?" Bobby swatted Andy with a bulging paper sac. "My lunch."

He bent over, nose to nose with Andy. Pinned him with a dark-eyed stare and hissed between gritted teeth, "You better think real hard about what you say next, baby. 'Less you're ready ta call me a thief and a liar. In public."

Andy gulped and shrank back. His eyes flashed around the room seeking a friendly face. Or a teacher. Or a way out.

Bobby straightened. "Huh. Didn't think so." He swaggered away to join his friends.

Andy sank into the nearest empty seat. His heart thudded in his ears so loud he didn't hear much of the assembly program. His neighbor prodded him to stand for the Pledge of Allegiance. He mumbled his way through 'America the Beautiful' forgetting half the words. The teacher had to call his name twice before he rose on shaking legs to follow her to his new classroom.

Somebody left a half a tuna sandwich in his desk at afternoon recess. Strange, 'cause it smelled just like his mom's tuna salad. But even though his stomach growled with hunger at the delicious combination of tuna, chopped celery and homemade mayo, he had trouble choking it down.

Andy stowed his new pencils, scribblers and workbooks in his desk. His wooden, roll-top pencil case gleamed. His rainbow of new pencil crayons were sharp, ready for map-making or decorating his crisp, new, brown-paper text book covers. But all the joy had leached out of his day. Even the sun seemed pale and listless.

Somehow he made it through the rest of the afternoon. Stumbled home and dropped his bookbag on the kitchen table. Andy hung up his shirt and pants, ready for another day, and changed into a clean t-shirt. Then he washed the last of the grit from his hands and knees.

He climbed up on the sink in his t-shirt and underpants to reach the medicine cabinet. Grabbed the bottle of peroxide his mom kept there and dabbed it on the freshly-bleeding cuts and gouges. Tears rolled down his cheeks as the peroxide bubbled and burned. If he'd known any really bad words, he'd have said them.

Once the burn faded, he stuck Band-Aids over the worst bits and pulled on his dungarees.

When his mom came home, she found him sitting at the kitchen table staring at his spelling homework.

His mom hung up her hat and coat and patted Andy's head. Opened the fridge and looked inside.

"How was your first day, Sweetie?"

"Not so good."

"Why? What happened?"

Andy could tell his mom hadn't had a very good day either. Her voice sounded kind of chokey, as if she was trying not to cry.

"You hungry?" she asked.

Andy shook his head.

"Me neither. Soup and crackers?"

Andy nodded. A tear slid down his cheek.

His mother stared. Knelt by his chair. "Sweety, what's wrong?"

Andy threw himself into his mother's arms and buried his face against her neck. "I lost it," he wailed. Tears were falling in earnest now. "My lunch box. I lost it." Between snuffles and sobs he told her about falling, about his skinned knees, about coming home without his lunchbox. But not a word about Bobby Burroughs. Years later, he would wonder why. But she didn't ask him then how he'd lost his treasure, so Andy didn't say.

"Oh, my poor boy. We're quite the pair, aren't we?"

Andy wiped his face on his t-shirt sleeve and stared at his mom.

She gave a little laugh. "I lost something today, too -- well, lost out on something."

"You didn't get the job as Head Teller?"

She shook her head. "They brought a man in from another branch."

Andy scowled. "That's not fair."

"No, it isn't. But life isn't fair, Andy. We just have to do the best we can with what we're given."

Andy's scowl deepened. He wasn't sure how, but he was gonna fix things for his mom. So she wouldn't have to work so hard at the bank. Maybe he'd become a famous cowboy and sell his own lunchboxes for a pile of money. Yeah, that'd be swell. Andy Anderson, the Arizona Ranger.

Soup and crackers tasted pretty good after all. Andy was still plotting his shiny new future when his mom tucked him in for the night.

"G'night, Sweetie. Happy trails, little buckaroo." She ruffled his hair and flipped his bedroom light off, then turned on the nightlight in the hallway so they be able to see their way to the bathroom at the head of the stairs.

Andy grinned and snuggled under his blankets. "G'night, Mom. Happy trails."

Senior Prom

Bobby Burroughs slouched against the bottom bleacher at the back of the school gym listening to the Glee Club warm up. He brushed at a smear of dust on the sleeve of his jacket. It wasn't quite up to Easy Rider standards. The long fringes down both arms were cool, but the pale leather was a bitch to keep clean. And trying to wipe it clean with his hand wasn't working. The jacket had yet to develop the patina of age and long use, so the early signs of wear just made it look grubby.

This'd be his last assembly, thank God. Not that God had played much of a part in Bobby's life to this point, let alone in his high school years. Not as far as Bobby was concerned. God had been as absent from his life as his father. There

239

one day to drop him and his mom off at church, Sunday School for four-year-old Bobby, and gone that afternoon.

It had taken Bobby a while to catch on. Before he figgered out what 'vacationing upstate' meant. That and the pitying looks from his Auntie Roma. He'd put paid to his cousins' sniggering damn fast though. Assholes. Their dad, Bobby's Uncle Burt, was no better'n Bobby's dad -- he just hadn't been caught. Yet.

Maybe his cousins were right, workin' with their dad. Al Jr. and Ralphie made good money. Always had nice clothes. Flash cars. But Bobby had other plans for his life. He was gonna get out of this jerkwater town. See the world before the draft caught up with him. Bobby wasn't sure how much he'd get to see in two years but he was damn sure gonna try for it all.

His duffle bag was already packed and stowed under his bed at home. His bike was gassed up and ready to go. Just the final certificate presentations an' speeches, then senior prom tonight and he was gone. He listened as the Glee Club wound up their plodding rendition of "America the Beautiful" and swung into the medley of old fifties ballads the music teacher deemed suitable for public consumption.

He'd heard them practicing the theme from "Hair" and "Crystal Blue Persuasion." He'd hoped they'd bust out some of those for the graduation ceremony, but it didn't sound as if they were on the conductor's list. *Oh, well, maybe for prom.* He pushed himself to his feet. Patted his shirt pocket. The reassuring crinkle of a plastic baggy told him the doobie he'd scored from Al Jr. was still safe. Bobby had big plans for tonight.

He slid round the end of the bleachers and stared to the kids on stage. At his girl, Elaine O'Connell, beautiful Lainie, a total fox, her luscious pink lips moist and parted in song, sharing a music folder with that damn Anderson doofus. Bobby's mouth quirked in a rare smile, *Lunch box boy.*

It had been a while since he'd thought about that. After Bobby'd made it home with his stolen treasure all those years ago, he'd washed out the thermos and stuffed it back in gaudy tin box. Hid it in the back of his closet, terrified his mom would see it, and make him give it back. It'd been there ever since, burning a hole in him like some damn tin conscience every time he opened his closet door -- his personal Jiminy Cricket. And leaving part of the loser's lunch for him hadn't salved it much.

Bobby wondered if Anderson even remembered the friggin' thing.

Tonight, though -- well, tonight would be a different story. Tonight he'd finally get past second base with Luscious Lainie. Fitting for his last night in town. First stop the Grand Canyon. Next stop San Fran. He ran a hand through his dark brown mane. Almost shoulder-length. He figgered he'd be okay with a flower in it if it'd score him some free love. *Yeah -- Haight-Ashbury here I come.* Bobby had a feeling he'd fit right in in Baghdad by the Bay.

On his way out the wide double doors, he paused for a quick look 'round. The prom committee had done a decent job on the decorations. The giant blow-up of a full moon outlined in silver sparkled against royal blue drapes at the back of the stage. One of the science nerds had taped a big red "X" on the crater where the July moon shot was suppose to land. If they even made it there. The grad class's theme "Aim High" was splashed across the dozens of banners hanging from the high ceiling, waving gently in time with the ceiling fans.

The theme had been controversial. A few of the teachers were dead set against all the money the government was sinking into NASA and the space race. But the kids had fought hard and won. And even Bobby had to admit, it made for a way-cool color scheme.

A huge arch of silver and blue balloons spanned the stage. The tables spaced round the sides of the gym were decked out with royal blue covers, tied up with white and silver ribbon bunting. The basketball hoops were raised and long nets crammed with blue and white and silver balloons were strung between them, ready for the midnight drop. Not too shabby for a stinky ol' school gymnasium.

• • •

By the time Bobby made it back with Lainie, the dance was well underway. Mr. O'Connell had insisted on driving them right up to the doors.

"It's almost the last time I'll ever drive my little girl to school. Well, 'til her own Graduation, next year."

Not that he'd driven her to school since round about Grade Eight. Or Bobby would never have met her. For sure, her dad would have chased off the shaggy-haired bad boy with the roll-cuff jeans and turned up shirt collar.

But Lainie had smiled. "Awe, Daddy, that's so sweet. We don't mind, do we Bobby?"

One look into those melting brown eyes and, of course, he hadn't minded. Not one little bit. He'd held hands with Lainie in the back seat. Careful to keep it hidden under her out-spread bouffant skirt. He caressed her palm with his thumb and tried to slide his hand under her thigh. She let out a nervous giggle and Mr.

244

O'Connell glanced up at the rear-view, sharp-eyed, suspicious. Bobby released her fingers and straightened his tie. Reminded himself there'd be plenty of time later.

The gym was crowded, Mo-Town standards blasting at ear-drum-rupture level. Shards of light from a giant mirror ball spangled the ceiling and walls, cascaded across the kids on the dance floor in a swirling, multi-colored shower of stars.

Bevies of tweenies with teased hair teetering in their first high heels fluttered from punch bowl to girls' washroom, shedding giggles and gossip along their unsteady way. Bobby cast a quick glance over the stag line -- the no-hopers standing along the back wall. Sure enough, there was Anderson and his fellow nerds, paper plates in hand, stuffing their faces with Ritz crackers and Cheetos. Pretending they didn't care about being dateless.

It was all Bobby could do to keep his hands in appropriate places while he and Lainie swayed on the dance floor, feet barely moving, to the strains of Bob Dylan's "Lay Lady Lay" and "This

Girl's in Love with you," delivered in Dionne Warwick's smoky treble. When the next record up was "This Girl is a Woman Now," Bobby pulled her from the gym into a darkened hallway.

They made their way past the science lab to the janitor's corridor. Found a little alcove between the banks of lockers. She came into his arms, mouth sweet and soft. He fumbled under her dress top, nothing more than a pair of wide, shirred, cross-over straps. Finally Bobby peeled them off her shoulders, down to her waist, and froze, his brain repeating her name.

She's so -- beautiful. The word "beautiful" wasn't near close to enough, but it was all he had.

The bra she was wearing wasn't her usual chaste, white cotton armor-plate. This was a little lace number that left half her boobs bare, like some pictures he'd seen in Eddy's sex magazines. Bobby wondered if Mrs. O'Connell had ever come across it in Lainie's drawer. He only wondered for a second, though. She'd never've let Lainie out of the house if she'd seen it.

Bobby's breath sighed out. He was almost afraid to touch her 'til he remembered something he'd heard Eddy say about his girlfriend. He brushed a thumb across Lainie's dark nipples. They puckered at once and she moaned and leaned into him. But as he reached under her dress, and groped past her garter belt she stiffened.

Her mouth on his, she groaned. "No, Bobby, we can't."

He cupped her face in both hands. "Babe." He kissed her again. Soft and deep. "C'mon, babe."

This time, when he slid his hand into her panties, she pressed towards him. His palm against her warm, bare ass cheek sent an electric shock through him. She let out a little yelp, muffled against his teeth, and her thighs opened, trembling. He grabbed for his zipper, but stopped when he tasted salt tears.

He pulled away, confused. Didn't she want this as bad as he did?

Her eyes were squeezed shut, huge crystal drops rolling down her cheeks. But she pulled his head down, her mouth on his hot, urgent. "Not here. Not like this."

Thank you, baby Jesus. His knees weak with relief, Bobby thought fast.

"I know a place. C'mon."

He didn't know, not for sure, but it sounded good when he said it. She held her dress top over her chest with one hand and squeezed his fingers tight in her other as he pulled her towards the equipment locker. One of his buddy's had boasted about making out on the tumbling mats. Bobby guessed it'd be as good a place as any for a first time.

Fortune smiled on him. The janitor'd forgotten to lock up. Bobby pulled the door open and backed Lainie up against it. He lowered his mouth to hers. And fortune stopped smiling.

A long-fingered hand grabbed his shoulder and spun him backwards, away from Lainie. His leather soles gave no purchase on the well-polished floor. Bobby's feet flew up and he went down hard on his back, knocking the wind out of him. He lay gasping, waiting for his vision to clear. And heard a much-despised voice talking to Lainie.

"You sure you're okay? He didn't hurt you?"

Effing Anderson. I'm gonna kill him. Bobby staggered to his feet to see his nemesis with Lainie wrapped in his Glee Club jacket, a solicitous arm draped round her shoulders. He'd never thought of Lunch box boy that way before. He hadn't thought much about him at all, let alone as his nemesis. But Bobby knew in that instant they were somehow connected. Always had been.

He staggered to his feet. "Lainie." The hoarse croak he squeezed out didn't sound like his voice at all. "Wait."

Lainie turned. Gave him a tremulous smile. "I gotta go, Bobby."

She pulled up her dress top and smiled up at her singing partner, as if seeing him in a new light.

"Andy's gonna take me home."

"Lainie." Bobby's hand dropped to his side. He stared at it, unaware 'til just then he'd reached out to her.

Next thing he was aware of was standing at the top of Warner's Hill pissing down the embankment. The popular make-out spot overlooking town had been abandoned in favor of senior prom and the many after-parties sure to spring up once the fireworks were over.

The town put on a show every year, in the hope it'd signal the end of the festivities. As if that'd be enough to send a bunch of horny, half-cut teenagers home on a hot, late spring evening, after a night of slow-dancing and spiked punch.

Bobby pulled the tin lunch box from his duffel bag and glared at it while he took another pull from the bottle of rum he'd liberated from Uncle Burt's liquor cabinet. The lock had always been easy to pick, and Bobby and his cousins had been regular if uninvited guests since Bobby was eight. His uncle kept it so well-stocked he'd never missed a bottle or two. He sure hadn't yet. And if he did, he'd prob'ly blame Eddy or Ralph.

"Effing lunch box." Bobby set the box in on the ground by his bike's front tire. Straddled his machine and revved the throttle. The throaty rumble warmed his belly in a way the rum hadn't. He tossed back another slug of his uncle's twenty-year-old Appleton Reserve and rocked his bike back and forth. Lifted the front wheel and set it in the box. Imagined how great it'd feel to run over the painted horse and the cowboy sweethearts' smiling faces. Mash 'em flat. Leave it on Anderson's porch as a grad gift. *Happy trails, Asshat*.

In the end though, he picked up the little tin box and stuffed it in his duffle-bag. Strapped the bag on his bike. Took one last, long pull from the bottle and hucked it over the guard rail into the darkness. Laughed when he heard it smash on the rocks below.

"Fuck you all, ya bunch a' losers," he yelled. And roared off into the night.

Diagnosis

"Mrs. Anderson, did you hear me?"

The doctor's voice was kind. Reassuring. But it echoed in Lainie's head, bounced around behind her eyes, distorted. Fading in and out so she couldn't make out the words. *What had she said?*

Lainie put out her hand to stop the voice, pleased to see her fingers were steady.

Her doctor's face swam into view. "Can I get you something? Some water?"

Lainie laughed. Clapped a hand over her mouth before it turned into a sob. *Or a scream.* She shook her head. "Maybe something stronger?" *Good, that was good. Humor always helps. Puts people at ease.* Lainie wondered why she was trying to put her doctor at ease.

The doctor's smooth, youthful face creased in a tiny smile. She waved a hand towards the water cooler, her eyes questioning.

Lainie forced her mouth into an upward curve. "No water. Thank-you." *Much better. That sounded almost natural.*

Lainie's doctor pushed the box of tissue to the front of her desk. "I'm sorry. This must be a shock. I know we were hoping for a better result."

I will not cry, I will not cry, I will not cry. Lainie stared at her clasped hands. A web of ropy blue veins stood out under her shiny, translucent skin, harsh against white knuckles. The nicks and scars a mute testament to the IVs and blood-lettings that had been her life for so many years. *God, my hands look like shit. A blotchy bundle of bones -- old lady hands at forty-seven.*

Finally, her lips moved, framing the first denial. "But I thought I was clean. You said I was clean. The last test --"

"I'm sorry, Lainie. We hoped so, too. But the last test was inconclusive. That's why we ran the second blood panel." The kind voice was firm. Lainie knew from experience, its warmth would cool with the next denial. And the next, until all that would be left was a kind of detached, clinical compassion.

I can't do this again. This would be her third round, puking her guts out while the drugs burned their way through her, killing everything in their path. Except, it seemed, their target.

The first time, she'd been clean for almost five years. The second, less than two. And now --

Then, it hit her. *Oh God, how can I tell Andy?* Her face crumpled and the tears came. She reached for the tissue box.

"I'll give you a moment." The doctor started to rise.

Lainie blew her nose and shook her head. "No, I'm alright."

Her oncologist sank back into her chair.

Lainie drew in a long, trembling breath. Exhaled and squared her shoulders. "Okay. What's next? When do we start?"

The doctor held Lainie's eye. "I'm sorry, Lainie."

Lainie stopped breathing. Her world contracted to the doctor's mouth framing the words 'I'm sorry.'

Lainie blinked, swallowed hard, and the doctor's office snapped back into focus. A pleasant room facing a charming garden two floors below. Comfortable padded chairs. Soft grey walls with a cheerful picture of a poppy field in summer behind the chrome and glass desk. The petals so delicate, so life-like, Lainie could all but see them bobbing gently in the warm breeze wafting down the hill towards her.

Somehow she choked out the words. "There's nothing?"

Again, the sad finality of tone and look. "I'm so sorry."

Lainie rose and walked to the door. She couldn't feel her feet on the floor and her fingers were numb, but she managed to turn the knob. Lainie registered a voice. Her doctor was saying something. Lainie turned. "I'm sorry?"

Reflex politeness -- what in hell am I sorry about?

"I said, 'When you're ready, I can give you some numbers. Contacts for when you want to make your -- arrangements."

Oh, fuck this. Lainie bolted from the office.

She called Andy several hours later from a low-ceilinged dive bar in a run-down part of town neither of them frequented. She must've walked there, but she didn't remember. And with a bit of luck and some determined drinking, she wouldn't remember much of the rest of her day, either.

She stared around the narrow room, at the shabby red leatherette booths and worn brown carpet. More holes and threadbare bits than the shag pile of its long-gone glory days. If it'd ever had any glory days. Lainie doubted it. Prob'ly sprang from its first bloom of youth straight to middle-aged decrepitude. *Like me.* Lainie gave herself a mental shake.

Stop being, morbid, my girl. It's party time!

The gin in her martini had arrived with no olives and an oily scum on top, so she'd switched to vodka after the first couple of drinks. Or maybe it'd been three. She wasn't sure. But the vodka was barely palatable.

She was contemplating going all in on Tequila shooters. She'd called Andy on the bar phone and was debating Tequilas with a friendly stranger on the next stool when Andy picked up.

Her cheery greeting was loud. Maybe a bit out of character, but she was sure Andy would be so relieved to hear from her he wouldn't care. "Hey, babe, how's it hangin'?" *Shades of high school.*

The shocked silence emanating from the other end of the line made Lainie giggle. She tried again. "How'd your meeting go, lover boy?"

"Lainie? Is that you?" Andy's incredulous reply was so typical of Andy she almost burst out laughing. Then she thought, "*Well, what the hell.*" So she did. The friendly stranger joined in.

"Lainie, where are you?"

Andy's voice was way too calm. *And even funnier. He's such a funny guy.*

She choked out the address between bouts of laughter. By the time Andy arrived, though, nothing was funny anymore. She collapsed, sobbing, in his arms.

Andy gathered up her coat and handbag. Thanked the bartender and left him a generous tip. Glared at the friendly stranger who offered to help, and then tried to cadge a ride. If her head hadn't been in such a muddle, Lainie would have made Andy drive the man home -- or wherever. She flapped a hand at the bartender and her new friend as Andy bundled her into the back seat. Then, finally, mercifully, the world went away.

• • •

'The desert is calm and peaceful and I am not' Lainie scratched out the words and started again. 'The desert is -- is' She stopped. *The desert is -- what? It just is. It's big, it's hot, and it's full of sand. It's a fucking desert.*

She tossed her journal aside. She hated journaling. It didn't make things better. It didn't bring her perspective. Trying to write out her feelings just left her hot and hostile. Andy's mom had suggested she give it a try. And Andy's mom was the kindest, most loving, supportive woman Lainie had ever known, so she'd tried. Lainie never felt that kindness more than when her own mom passed. Lainie supposed she should be grateful now, too. Except she didn't feel grateful. Not one bit.

Mrs. Anderson had suggested the trip. Found the rental, made all the arrangements. She probably needed a rest from the shouting matches as much as Andy and Lainie did.

That's all they seemed to do now. Nothing was ever right or good enough. All she did was pick at Andy. Pick, pick, pick. Lainie hated herself for it, but the harder he tried to be loving and supportive, the more she lashed out.

"I don't know what you want from me any more, Lainie," he'd shouted one night, goaded out of all patience by her constant, snide digs about incompetent men. "Just tell me what you want and I'll do it."

"Stop trying to make me feel better. I want a husband not a fucking shrink," she'd yelled. "I want -- I want our lives to go back to normal. I want to not die."

It was unfair. She knew it was unfair. *But so was life -- or death in this case*.

Andy'd had no answer for that. No one did.

So here they were, baking in the Nevada sun, trying to salvage some shred of kindness between them, if not love. Trying to find solid ground where they could regroup and move forward through all of this. *'All of this'* -- *'all of this' is what's left of my life. I want it to be more than 'all of this.'*

Andy set a tray on the glass table beside her and adjusted the huge umbrella to better shade her from the scorching sun. He'd been tiptoeing around for days, waiting for the next explosion. Waiting for her to go off the rails again.

He carried her glass to the edge of the patio and decanted the melted ice into a round, hand-painted clay pot holding some kind of sword-leafed plant. He set the glass on the table and re-filled it from the pitcher. Fat drops of condensation rolled down sides of the colorful hand-painted glass pitcher to leave a wet mark on the tray cloth. Crisp and white, fresh-pressed like Andy's t-shirt. Like everything else in this house ---- in this *hacienda*, she corrected herself -- crisp and pressed and hand-painted.

If I see one more hand-painted anything I swear I will fucking scream.

Andy spotted her journal face-down on the patio where it had landed. He flashed her a shy smile -- one part patience, one part I-love-you, and two parts are-you-going-to-flip-out-again? He strolled over to the little book and bent to retrieve it. As his hand touched the journal he sneaked a furtive glance at Lainie.

She'd been waiting for it and pinned him with a basilisk stare. *Caught ya checkin' up, bud. Don't ever fuck with Sheena, Bitch Queen of the Desert.*

Andy's eyes winced away from her baleful gaze. But he retrieved the journal and set it on the table beside her. Folded himself into his lounge chair and picked up his pocket book. Pretended to read as if nothing had happened.

Lainie felt something snap. She grabbed the pitcher from the table and dumped it over Andy's head then threw it against the hand-painted tiles surrounding the fire pit in the middle of the terrace. She barely heard the crash of the

261

glass as it shattered into hundreds of tiny, exquisite, hand-painted fragments. She stared into Andy's stunned, dripping face and screamed. As loud and as long as she could. Over and over and over 'til her throat burned and she was dizzy and gasping for breath. Then she spun on her heel and raced for her bedroom. Slammed the door and collapsed on the bed, dry-eyed, her head spinning.

The only sound in the room beside her ragged breathing was the muted tick of the alarm clock on the bedside table. Lainie'd purged all their clocks at home. She couldn't bear the relentless reminders of time flying by. Precious minutes slipping through her fingers. But Andy'd pleaded with her to keep one, just so they wouldn't miss the train, or their next flight to wherever they were planning to visit to kill some more time.

She listened to the sounds of sweeping, of glass shards tinkling into the waste-basket. Hand-painted, no doubt. The shower running in the guest bedroom. Then the quiet creak of the linen closet opening and closing. Footsteps in the hallway. A tentative tap on her bedroom door.

"Lainie?"

She didn't answer. Couldn't. Hadn't a clue what to say to pull them back from the abyss.

Andy walked over and sat on the bed. Pulled her onto his lap and nuzzled her hair.

She leaned into him, her hand on his chest, the heat of his body seeping into hers, feeling his warm breath in her hair, the strong steady beat of his heart. "God, you smell good."

"Lainie --"

She raised her head.

Tears streamed down Andy's cheeks. "I love you so much. I can't -- I can't lose you like this before you're even gone." His voice broke.

She pulled his head down and kissed him. Tasted his tears as they rolled into her mouth. "I love you, too, baby." She clung to him, sobbing. And finally, the words came.

"Andy, it was so kind of your mother to arrange this for us, but I can't just sit here and wait to die. I want us to do something. Have some fun together. Now. While I still can. I want you to look at my picture after I'm gone and say, 'Damn, we had some good times.' "

Andy's arms tightened round her.

"Can we do that, Andy -- can we go ride a monster roller-coaster? Eat too much ice cream? Go see silly things like the world's biggest ant farm at that gas station outside Sonoma?"

Andy nodded. Unable to speak.

"Good." Lainie smiled. "Still love me?"

Andy nodded again, blinking through his tears. "Always"

"Good. Then shut the fuck up and make love to me. Like you mean it, goddamit. I'm not made of glass. I won't fucking break."

She didn't have to ask twice.

It was twilight by the time they surfaced. The desert was painted with purple shadows, long-fingered and mysterious, turning blazing day into streaks of orange and peach and palest gold over a misty indigo horizon. A hint of ozone tingled in the air, promising another midnight rain shower.

Lainie stretched and rubbed a foot against Andy's long leg. A rush of joy flooded through her.

My god, I love this man.

She arched her back and grinned up at him. "Not bad for an old guy."

He ran a hand down her belly and smiled as her skin shivered under his touch.

"It's early yet." He waggled an eyebrow. Wicked, suggestive.

Lainie laughed. "Food first. Sex later -- more sex later," she amended.

Andy's hand continued it's downward quest. "Later?"

A little sigh escaped her lips, then she giggled. "Oh, all right, food later."

• • •

Some weeks after their desert stop-over, they were passing a second-hand shop in a small northern California town. One of those not-too-touristy places with restaurants where the locals ate and tiny, main street coffee shops with bright flower baskets hanging by their doors. Places where proud owners brewed real cappuccino and baked their own bread and pastries.

"Andy, look. I haven't seen anything like this in forever." Lainie pointed to a display of memorabilia from the nineteen-fifties. TV heroes. A Gene Autry poster and autographed records. Plastic figurines of the Lone Ranger and Tonto. Zorro astride his black stallion.

And in the middle of the display, a tin lunch box with Dale Evans and Roy Rogers and Trigger the Wonder Horse.

Andy stared. The thermos was missing, and the paint was worn and chipped. One of the metal clasps was broken. But it was unmistakeable. Just like the one he'd lost. He smiled, remembering his dreams of becoming a famous cowboy.

Instead, he'd become a successful accountant. Bought a house for his mom. She still lived in it. She'd retired from the bank a while ago, though. As branch manager. She'd be waiting to welcome them home, whenever he and Lainie returned.

Lainie linked her arm through his. "Penny for them, mister."

Andy smiled. "I used to have a lunch box like that. I'll tell you about it sometime." They both knew he'd probably forget, but that was alright. They strolled off into the warm summer afternoon, down the wide, tree-lined main street in search of the perfect place for supper.

Homecoming

Andy leaned back on the wrought iron park bench, the pale afternoon sun warm on his face. Spring crocuses were just starting to poke their heads above the ground along the edges of the cobbled walkways. Here and there, in the shadows under huge elm trees, patches of snow clung to the ground but they'd be gone soon enough. And with any luck, so would the cold winds funneling that damn Canadian Arctic cold-front down stateside. One export Andy wished the toque-wearing Canucks would keep to themselves.

Andy spotted an old man ambling down the bike path towards him. He'd noticed the homeless man before scrounging through the park's waste bins. Surprised him early one morning, asleep on a bench, covered in newspapers. Threadbare overcoat, raggedy too-big pants. The man's last shred of pride showed in his worn but well-cared-for work boots.

Today, though, the old guy was with another man. Taller, younger. Better kept. His jeans and t-shirt were clean, at least. His jean jacket was covered in crests and patches -- bike clubs, rallies, music festivals, down both sleeves as well as the back and front. Whoever the guy was, he'd seen a lot of the country. He carried a bulging satchel slung over one shoulder, and looked a year or so older than Andy. Andy didn't recognize the man's weathered face, but there was something familiar about him.

Jean-jacket was talking with the old man, trying to convince him to come with him. He held out a folded piece of paper, but the old man shook his head. Finally, Jean-Jacket pulled a wax-paper-wrapped sandwich out of his satchel and offered that, too. The old guy sniffed the sandwich kinda suspicious, then stuck out his other hand. Jean-Jacket smiled and pulled out an apple and a pair of work socks.

The old man stowed the socks in one pocket, the apple in another, and shambled off without a backwards glance.

Jean-Jacket shook his head with a rueful smile and headed for Andy's bench. Plunked down at the other end. "Mind if I join you?"

Andy shook his head with a smile. "Free country."

Jean-Jacket chuckled. "No such thing as a free lunch, though."

Andy laughed. "That why your friend turned you down?"

Jean-Jacket grinned. "Ol' Dougie? Nah, we don't preach at them. He jus' knew we'd make him take a bath. Dougie doesn't like baths. Says it'll wash off his protective coating." He flicked a glimmering sidelong glance at Andy. "After all his years living rough, it'll take more'n one bath to scrub that ol' hide clean."

Jean-Jacket rubbed a work-roughened hand through his short-cropped thatch, dark brown shot through with silver. Like Andy's, closing in on more silver than brown. He set his satchel on the bench between them and opened the flap. "Sandwich?"

He poked the wax-paper-wrapped parcels. "We got ham, cheese, ham and cheese, PB&J, and mystery meat." He winked at Andy. "I'd pass on the mystery meat, I were you. I think it's liver paste but even the stray cats won't eat it."

Andy shook his head. "Thanks, I've already eaten."

Jean-Jacket grinned and chowed down on a PB&J. "You come here often?" he asked around a mouthful of sandwich. Wiped some crumbs off his chin and swallowed. "Sorry. Don't often get to sit and chat."

Andy's mouth quirked. "Too busy rounding up strays?"

"Something like that." Jean-Jacket wolfed down the rest of his sandwich and wiped his hands on a paper napkin. Picked up his satchel and glanced around the park. "Looks like most of the regulars have already headed uptown to catch the office crowd. Not bad pickings on a payday Friday, Which this is. Better get down there and see if I can feed a few more."

He rose and stuck out his hand. "Thanks for the company. I'm Rob, by the way."

"Andy. Andy Anderson."

Something flickered in the man's eyes. Gone before Andy could put his finger it.

Rob nodded. "See you 'round." He headed off across the park with a long easy stride.

Andy stared after him. A memory fizzed in the back of his mind, trying to poke through the half-million items on his mental to-do list now it was tax season again. Nothing popped, though. Andy shook his head and frowned. *Oh well, seemed like a good guy.*

Andy checked his watch. Better get moving if he wanted to have dinner with Mom. It'd take a while to get across town in the Friday traffic, and the lodge insisted on a strict schedule for everything. No exceptions, even for frequent visitors.

He'd wanted to move his mother in with him after Lainie passed. The house felt too big and empty. But his mother had smiled. Patted his hand. "You're still a young man, Andy. You don't need an old lady underfoot cramping your style."

Andy'd shaken his head. "Fifty-two's not young, Mom, and you're not an old lady."

But she'd been adamant. When she was ready to give up her house a year or so later, she'd moved into the lodge. Andy had to admit, she loved it there with her girlfriends. Monday bridge club, Tuesday movie nights, and almost daily excursions to coffee shops, and the local malls. His mother had a busier social life than he did.

Andy smiled as he headed across the street to the office to collect his car. Whistled a snatch of a tune under his breath. He stopped for a moment and cocked his head, trying to place it. *Whatever it was, it had a nice lilt*. He'd have to ask his mother. She'd probably remember.

He whistled another bar and then he had it. "Happy Trails," the theme from the Roy Rogers Show. He slid into the driver's seat and checked his rearview. Wondered why the tune had popped into his mind after all these years. Then forgot about it as he navigated the crowded roads already filling with Friday evening traffic.

• • •

It was mid-summer before Andy ran into Rob again. He'd stopped by the park across the street a few times thinking he might see Rob there with his satchel full of sandwiches, chasing down another stray. Andy felt a tenuous connection, but wasn't quite sure why. After all, they'd barely met.

This afternoon was different, though. Andy had finally kept his promise to Lainie and dug out the rolls of film they'd taken on their travels. He'd just got them back from the developer and was sitting on his usual bench with the dozen or so packets of photos, nerving himself to go through them. He leaned back and closed his eyes. The dappled light of the summer sun filtering through the wide-spreading boughs of the graceful elms was warm on his face.

The park bench creaked and flexed under the weight of another body. Andy kept his eyes closed, hoping whoever it was would think he was asleep and move along. *No such luck.* The bench creaked again as his companion settled into a more comfortable position. Andy stifled a sigh and opened his eyes. Shot a sideways glance in the direction of his seat-mate.

"Sorry to disturb you," the man offered.

To Andy's relief, it was Rob. Andy smiled. "No worries."

Rob gestured towards the photo envelopes clutched in Andy's hand. "Been traveling?"

"What?" Andy stared at packets. Realised he hadn't unsealed a single flap. "No, these are from years ago. I just -- I haven't looked at them yet."

Rob cocked his head. "Why not?"

Andy frowned.

Rob sat back, concern replacing his curiosity. "Sorry. It's not my business."

Andy shook his head. "No. It's okay."

He took a deep breath, unsure where to start at first. He took out at the first photo and the dam burst. He talked for the better part of an hour. Telling Rob about Lainie. Her diagnosis, their travels. He showed Rob photos of all the wonderful, crazy things they'd seen and done. The World's Largest Ant Farm. The Smallest Desert. The giant redwoods. Big Sur. The Maine sugar bush in autumn -- ablaze in scarlet and gold. A huge collection of hand-crocheted doilies in Sioux City. An alien landing pad in Vulcan, Alberta, Canada, complete with Star Trek character cutouts and a landing-craft-shaped ice cream parlor. Best ice cream in the country. His and Lainie's last five years together captured on a few rolls of film. Too few rolls. Too few years.

Andy reached the end of the pictures. And his stories. The men sat for a moment, neither willing to break the silence. At last, Andy sighed and returned the photos to their envelopes.

Rob reached into his satchel and pulled out an old-fashioned, child's tin lunch box. "Lainie was a special lady. You'll need somewhere special to keep those pictures."

Rob opened the box and removed a well-worn, slip of paper. Folded and refolded many times, from the look of it. Andy glimpsed what it said before Rob tucked it in his jacket pocket. Printed in block letters, the note read 'Lunch-box boy.'

A shock fizzed through him. *Rob was Bobby Burroughs?*

Rob caught Andy's glance. His hand rested on the pocket for a moment. "Yeah -- I told myself I didn't remember your name. For a long time I didn't want to." He flashed a lop-sided grin.

"I spent a lot a' years running from my past -- trying to drown it. Damn near drowned myself before I finally figured out I couldn't run forever. Like that sad old punchline. 'Every time I turn around, there I am.' " He shook his head. "I was an asshole. I blamed you for troubles of my own making. I'm sorry, Andy. For everything."

He set the lunch box on the bench beside Andy.

Bemused, Andy picked up the little tin box. He ran his hand over the smiling faces of the cowboy sweethearts and Trigger the Wonder Horse, their vivid colors just starting to fade. For a second, the old feelings of shame and inadequacy washed over him. At once replaced by stronger, better memories -- the warmth of Lainie's hand in his when they'd spotted that other lunch box in the antique store; the love in his mother's voice as she checked the band-aids on his skinned knees all those years ago.

"Someone must have needed it a lot more than you did, Sweetie. But if it's meant to be yours, it'll come home again. I promise."

He flicked a glance at Rob. "Won't you need this for other amends?"

Rob's eyes twinkled. "I tend not to save them so long these days. Best to deal with 'em right away."

Andy's mouth quirked. He undid the clasps and laid the packets of photos inside, then reclipped the little box. *Welcome home*. He gave the lid a pat and nodded to Rob. "Thank you."

Rob stood up. "Thank you, Andy." He stuck out his hand.

Andy looked up. When he thought about it afterwards, he had no idea where the words sprang from, but he was glad he'd said them. "If you're not busy Friday, my mom would enjoy meeting you. Come for supper."

Rob stared. Then a slow smile spread across his face. He blinked and ducked his head, wiped a hand across his mouth. When he looked up his eyes were shining. "Thank you. I'd like that very much."

The two men shook hands. Rob headed off across the park. Andy sat for a moment, his hand on the lunch box. Then he tucked it under his arm and strode towards his office and his parked car. The spring in his step had been missing for some time. But it was back now. And the lilting tune he whistled floated behind him on the warm summer air.

'Happy trails to you, 'til we meet again'

• • •

Acknowledgements

Thanks so much to my friend and incredible editor, Susan Brearley. Without your support and guidance, this would never have been possible. Thank you to The Garden for helping this woman find and share her voice. And thank you to all my online friends and fellow writers—so kind and supportive, but also always truthful.

Bless you, my sisters—my earliest beta readers—Nonie and Annie, you waded through years of revisions, rewrites, and begin-agains with grace and compassion. Your encouragement kept me writing.

Thanks to Sandy Knight, Aura Wilming and Geoff Atkins of "Hinged" for the encouragement and truly stellar prompts which inspired so many of these tales.

I hope this collection brings you joy, helps you pass a pleasant hour or two, and gives you something to think about. If you enjoy reading it even half as much as I enjoyed the writing, then I've done my job. Happy trails.

About the Author

A.L. (Elle) Fredine has been writing since Moses was in short pants, honing her craft online since 2008. Her work under the name 'Elle Fredine' has been included in several print anthologies and featured in online publications. Her recent work is available on Medium.

A.L. is an accomplished artist, poet, and educator, editor for five online publications, with thirty-plus years directing and designing for the theatre. Writing as A.L. Fredine, she has recently published an anthology of short stories and is working on two romance-mystery novels: one contemporary and one Edwardian.

About This Edition

This first edition of *The Lunchbox: A Collection of Short Stories* was published in 2025
by **Garden of Neuro Publishing Company**, a New York nonprofit corporation.

The text is set in Century Gothic, a geometric sans-serif typeface designed by Monotype in 1991. Known for its clean lines and modern elegance, Century Gothic offers excellent readability.

Cover art by Susan Brearley.

Cover design by Stefanie Morejon.

Printed in the United States of America and Canada.

Citations:

1. *"Requiem" is Robert Louis Stevenson's self-written epitaph, 1880*

2. *In the best tradition of fairytales, the name "Holzfaller" translates to "woodcutter."*

3. *"Homeward Bound" by Paul Simon, January 19, 1966, released by Columbia Records*